SUMMER
ROUNDS

Praise for B.G. Bradley's *Winter Heart*
The first in the Hunter Lake Series...

"There's love in every sentence."

–Beverly Matherne

Poet and Author of *Bayou des Acadiens (Blind River)*

"B.G. Bradley is that rare storyteller who seems to speak to each of us, secretive and universal, like a whisper against firelight. The truth of nature feels absolutely alive on the page. I can't wait for the next visit, or perhaps I should say, visitation.

"Like his beloved Upper Peninsula, Bradley's Winter Heart *is gently personable, persuasive and funny, and rooted into steadfast rock underneath."*

–Shelley Russell, PhD,

Author of the Kennedy Center Award-winning *Haywire* and other plays

*"*Winter Heart *is one of those hauntingly earnest books that stays with you long after you've read the final chapter. Every place has a spirit – that's what I believe – and B.G. Bradley perfectly captures the spirit of the book's setting, the "U.P.", the Upper Peninsula of Michigan. I've never been to the U.P.! But I know with certainty what like is like there now."*

–Arvid Nelson

Creator of the hit graphic novel series *Rex Mundi* and *Zero Killer*

"I don't know why, but often before beginning a book I thumb through it, read the blurb, the back cover, see if chapters have titles, and glance at a few pages. I guess it's like kicking the tires of a car before you buy it. Admittedly, it's as pointless as judging a book by its cover, but this time after a quick look through Winter Heart *my first thought was this will never work. I was wrong, utterly wrong.*

"The poetry intermingled throughout the novel is essential to its success, the paragraphs and whole pages in italics with words here and there in bold type work, and the strange way in which chapters are sometimes separated into small, often only a paragraph in length, Parts 1, 2, 3, etc. does not interrupt the flow of the book. So I am publicly eating crow and praising the author for his creative approach to writing and formatting this very satisfying novel.

"This is the first in the author's Hunter Lake series. I'm eagerly looking forward to the next."

–Tom Powers, Michigan in Books Review

www.michiganinbooks.blogspot.com

SUMMER ROUNDS

a novel by

B.G. BRADLEY

Benegamah
Press

Hulbert Lake, MI
Canby,OR

Benegamah Press
Hulbert Lake, Michigan
Canby, Oregon

Cover photo by B.G. Bradley
Cover and book design by Matt Dryer

Printed in the United States of America

For Matt Dryer, my younger brother-in-arms
in this nebulous battle called art.

FOREWORD
By B.G. Bradley

Dale wanted to talk. I know that sounds crazy, but that's the way it works. Artists of all kinds and actors and writers in particular hear voices of characters in their heads. I've been both an actor and a writer all my life, and many who know me will vouch for having seen the voices in my head spill over into real life, in the form of this old man mouthing esoteric words as he walks down U.P. trails, paddles his canoe, or pedals his ancient bike. My dogs have all come to take it for granted.

Anyway, Dale Sylvanus, the handyman and ex-Marine from my first published novel, oh yes, there have been others, but we'll get to that, wanted to talk. This happened about half way through the writing of Winter Heart, before I retired from teaching, before I reconnected with Matt Dryer, my publishing partner in Benegamah Press, when I was still trying to figure out what the ultimate fate of this latest novel would be. Would it just sit on a shelf like many of the others. Would I find a way to serialize this novel as I had in a newspaper column with two others. Or was there another way? Like I said, we'll get to all that.

I was a little miffed at Dale, because I still had a good deal of the first book to write and he was clamoring for the second. I was a little reluctant to let him talk, not only because I was already busy with writing something else, but because I was pretty sure that drywall, screw guns, trailer hitches, and battlefields in Iraq and Afghanistan, were going to come up. I know next to nothing about any of these things, but Dale assured me that he knew how to explain things like these to pencil pushers like me. Turns out, or at least I think it turns out, he was right. You be the judge. Anyway, he didn't baffle me with terms that confused me, when I finally did get around to hearing him out. And so, the second book in the Hunter Lake series, Summer Rounds, was born.

And so, here we are, at the second book in the series. Dale is through talking to me for a while, though you will hear from him again off and on in works yet to be published. In this work he takes you to a different part of Hunter and environs, though a few of the characters from the first book, Jen in particular, still inhabit it. He takes you here on a tour of the rougher side of Hunter, the side with dirt under the fingernails. The insights, though, are every bit as profound as anything in Winter Heart, I think. And the handy man even has something to say about the state of the journalistic world I once inhabited, and how it has come to be what it is now.

Most, surprising to me of all, though I suppose it shouldn't be, as a lifetime more-or-less Catholic, the book takes you into the moral world of a left wing priest. I didn't see that coming. I didn't really see any of this coming. I just listened to Dale, and let him tell the story. I had no idea where he was going. And the ride along the back roads around the town, down the river and around the lake, have been no less mysterious to me, than the rest of my life. So, thanks, for coming back for a second tour of Hunter Lake. I hope you'll be around for more. I don't know what's coming next, any more than you do.

I just keep listening to the voices.

-B.G. Bradley
August 2017

Only connect!
–E.M. Forster

You don't know about me…
–Mark Twain

Sunday, 6:37 a.m.

It's hot and my head hurts. Went to bed two hours ago. Nasty one. Church in 20 minutes or so. Told Father Bill I'd be there and talk to him after about the landscaping and the bathroom at the priest's house on College Hill in town…what's it they call priest's houses?…rectory, and some clean up at the, little lake church out here….St. Brigid's. I could skip church. Better not. Ma would be mad. Father Bill would give me that look. Jesus might not understand either.

Hughie. 'One more,' he says. Then when we've had eight each on my dime at the River House, he tells me he's got a fifth in his truck. 'River House', that's pretty fancy name for a run down old hotel and bar along the wild old water. It was quite the place once, Pop says. Needs fixin' bad. It's out north of Hunter off the river road above the hill. Anyway, back to last night, pretty soon that fifth is gone, so we come back here to the lake, takin' the back roads south around town all the way except for a half mile of M–28 before the lake turn, drink some warm ones of the old man's that he hides out here in the boathouse, so Ma won't be mad. He ain't much of a drinker at all, really. Never was, but he likes one now and then. Anyway, I wind up sleepin' under a canoe. Fuckin' Hughie.

Wonder if he's around here somewhere. Don't matter. Couldn't wake that fat slug if I tried. Okay. Okay. Push the hair back. Tuck in. How'm I lookin' in this old window? Woo… Couple a years, Dale Sylvanus, you got a couple a years on ya. And you ain't gettin' any slimmer. The red in the hair is goin' pretty gray too. Look about as old as Pop. Wonder if that's every day, or just today. You can blame it on the service all ya want, but that was 19 years ago mostly, then 4 years ago for that one crazy call up. They wouldn't have ya now. Wouldn't have ya. Good thing. Doubt I could hold a rifle straight. Doubt I could shoot at anybody. Really doubt that. That ain't the cause of this, though. That ain't the cause. Goin' to war right here couple nights a week… Okay, most nights, with Hughie and Shine and Chessy and Big Ol' for 19 years and even before that. Not so much Big Ol' lately, though, I notice, come to think of it. Anyway, that's the cause, Dale Sylvanus. Should listen to Father Bill more, and Ma, and pay attention when the old man kids me and puts in that hard look makes me feel like crap. And Carrie…well…sure…

Get walkin', Dale! Where's that Tylenol? Here it is. Here it is, right in the pocket of my rain coat. Rain water on it and the pills sticky as hell. Could go for just one shot…ooo… Drinkin' and cussin'. Tryin' to cut it back on both every day, but it's hard. Funny, when I'm around the Puppies, that's what Pop calls us… me and Hughie and the others…it don't seem that hard not to cuss. They started callin' me 'Padre' last spring when I started goin' back to Mass. It don't matter. Anyway, the cuss words have stopped comin' around the Puppies. I seem to only cuss now when I'm around customers. Then, I pretend they're comin' out by accident. They seem to get a charge outta that. 'Part of the act' like Pop says. 'If lake and river people think you're dumb, you'll likely make a profit out of it." When he says that he always gives that little good hearted laugh. The old man's a good sort, and he don't like foolin' people. What's more, he never made an unfair bargain with anybody in his life. But he gives the lake people what they want, a little, what's it?…local color… and he's right, ya do gotta make a livin'. And he's got a point about the summer people. Not all them people are the same though. There's enough hind ends in every walk of life to keep the world in stock of them, I guess. The Puppies are always talkin' about all them 'assholes from the college and the lake', but they ain't all hind ends. People surprise ya. People in every walk of life. Learned that in the service. Learned that from doin' my rounds around here. People surprise ya.

Glad I only gotta walk down the lake to get ta Mass. I like the little church by the lodge. "Your church too, Dale. Your church too. It's always waiting for you." That's what Father Bill says. I like to think that's true. The old man says it's been here since 1920's. Some a them Ohio lake folks built it for their minister, that had the camp up at Preacher's Point: Rev. Smithson. He was a Presbyterian, I think. He died; his family took over there. Then there weren't no more Holy Rollers in the Smithson family. So that was the end of church services out here for a while.

When Father Bill pulled in at the college in Hunter, seven, eight years back, Pop and Ma took him on a tour of the whole town, the river and the lake. He spotted the little church out here and thought it'd be just right for sunrise Mass in the summer. He gets ideas, ya know? And once he does he don't let go of 'em until they're finished. Anyway, he got in touch with all the movers and shakers out here through Pop and offered to fix up the place if it could be Catholic. They hadn't used it in 35 years and it was near fallin' down so they said okay. Some of 'em even come to Mass. Makes Pop laugh, "Old Mr. Chesterfield would fall down dead to think his great grand kids was Catholic!" Ma thinks it's pretty funny too, but she's nicer about it.

Ma. She's gonna be waitin' for me at church. She'll just smile and give me a peck on the cheek when I show up. She'll have Donny and Kelly with her too. I should be ashamed. I should be ashamed that Ma and Pop spend most of the time with my kids that I should be spendin' with 'em. I should be ashamed, but I get so busy with the rounds, I forget to be. Ma never says a word. Pop just spits and stares when I'm really bad. Mostly, he's cheerful, though. Tries to kid me back to bein' who I should be. He'll never give up, so I can't neither. My wife, Carrie gets along great with 'em both and she needs the time Ma and Pop give her by takin' care of the kids, to work at the hospital in Hunter. That ain't right that they should all have to do that. Ain't nobody's fault but mine. The kids are good, though. Way better than I ever was. I don't know... I don't know.

Water's been runnin' down the hills. Muddied up the lake. Bugs are out pretty bad. Ouch. That one came back bloody. Here we go now. Here we go. There's Father Bill. I can see him from here. Good number of cars in the old lake lodge parking lot. Used to be lots of cars here all summer, but ever since Ma and Pop retired from runnin' the Clear Water Lodge two years ago and the lake club shut the lodge down, that's changin'. Me and Dad are still on as the caretakers for the lake, though. Kinda like bein' a ghost sometimes, wanderin' around lookin' at empty cabins in the spring and fall, trudgin' out here in the winter.

Like I say, good crowd in the parking lot anyway, though. Not as many as when the bishop was here. That was a funny Sunday. There he was havin' everybody kiss his ring, big hat and all. Truth, I think Father Bill thought it was pretty funny too. That Father Bill is a character. Nobody else could talk the church into keeping this chapel goin'. Collection runs the power and they don't need any heat but the wood stove 'cause it only runs in summer when the college kids are mostly gone and the church in Hunter is closed.

Anyway, Pop and me fix what needs fixin' on the church free, so that's Father's argument for the Church. That and bringin' in more lake Catholics I guess. Truth is, he likes doing his sunrise Masses in the summer with the wind comin' in off the lake. Truth is he likes to hunt and fish too, so he likes the access out here. He fires up that little wood stove in the church to warm himself after ice fishin' sometimes. How he talked the bishop into keepin' this little church open when they're closin' up all over the U.P. I'll never know. Wonder if it had anything to do with the rich folks from Ohio and some donations the church might get...ha...I just wonder.

"Hello, Dale. Your Mom's inside with the kids. We'll talk after." Father Bill looks at me all kind of intense for a second under them snow white eyebrows. He runs a hand over his bald head. The other hand kinda fingers that old, old rosary stickin' out of his pocket from under his...what...vestments. Then he winks at me. He got that rosary from the last priest. Father Dennis. Every new priest here gets it. Ma says it came from the first missionary that was here. Used to have deer marrow string holdin' them beads together, Father says. The tribe give it to the first missionary way back in the 1800's I guess. That marrow musta rotted at some point er other. Somebody got serious then and strung'em back together on a pretty stout wire. Biggest rosary I ever seen. Kind of a...what's it...tradition...in Hunter, that rosary. I think most of the priests like it. Father Bill seems to. Anyway, if he didn't wear it pretty regular, the church ladies would be after him, wondering where it was.

"Sure, Father," I say. I half forgot what he said, but it don't matter. He'll be waitin' at the end of mass.

There they are. There they are, third pew back, just like always. Ma's smilin' at me. Kelly looks mad. Donny's hopin' we can go fishin' later. We'll see. We'll see.

Kelly, dressed in jean shorts and a tank top and sandals, looks out the side window towards the west end of the lake when I get into the pew. She looks like Carrie, thank God. Ma touches my shoulder, sweet and kind like always. Donny looks around Ma with that look that says, "Please, please…" Breaks my heart sometimes. Reminds me I ain't a prize. I ain't a prize. I know Carrie ain't tellin' the kids bad stuff about me. Nice of her. She sure could. She still loves me, least last time I checked. She says she'll always stay my wife, but she says she ain't livin' with me again till the stuff with The Puppies, Hughie and all the rest, stops. I told her I don't know when that's gonna be. She says, "Well, Dale, you tell me when, and you can come back that day, no questions asked."

I'm a damned fool not to take her up on it, but The Puppies, well, we've been together since kindergarten, then after me and Hughie went to war and I kinda come apart, they stayed by me. Seemed to bring us even closer. I feel like I owe'em, I don't know, friendship, no matter what they do. And, well, I don't want ta make Carrie no promises I can't keep. Love her too much for that. I know I'd tell her that was all over, and mean it too, and then a couple days later I'd run into one of'em and well, it's a small town. I don't know.

Should go to confession. Father Bill thinks so too. Won't though, I don't think. "Too proud" Ma says. Pop, in his kinda quiet way agrees with me, says nobody's got any business with what's in a man's head but the man. He was in Vietnam, think what he says has somethin' ta do with that. Makes sense it would. Course he ain't here, even though he was raised Catholic. Father Bill never asks about him. I figure Father figures if he raises it with the family Pop won't ever come to confession or to Mass, for that matter. That's probably good thinkin'. But Pop most likely ain't ever going to come anyway.

Thing about church is, you got two options way I see it.

The first way is you can try to focus in on what the priest's sayin'. If you do that, then you probably get more out of it, but the service takes forever. That's the one I should do and I never do. The other thing you can do, and it works better if you don't think about it and it just sorta happens, is ta get on a line'a thinkin'. About a project, or about somethin' that happened a long time ago, but nothin' about bein' with a girl or anything nasty like that 'cause then ya feel bad all Sunday and most of the way to Wednesday. Course, soon as you think that, that's all ya can think of, which is too bad. Sometimes I think God made us up kinda funny.

No, a better way is to just get thinkin' on some clean nice thought or about somethin' ya gotta do, and next thing you know yer walkin' up for communion, and you daydreamed through all the blessings over the bread and wine and what not. I always like when ya get to the Our Father, 'cause then ya know she's almost over. The best Mass of all time for me was once a few years back, when I come back to myself, with Father sayin' "The Mass is ended, go in peace" made me feel all light inside. Especially 'cause it took me by surprise. That only happened but once. Walkin' up in the Communion line and gettin' the Host almost always wakes me up. When I manage to daydream through Mass, it does surprise me, though, I feel light inside all day, 'cause it's like…I don't know…like God got in there without my lookin'. That's His best chance.

I wonder now. I wonder now what's gonna happen with Kelly. This ain't a good line of thought. Might get me through to the end of Mass, but I'll feel bad. Girls got it rough. Maybe Kelly more than other girls her age. She's 13. She's 'bout ready to be a woman, if she ain't already. Sad, I don't know exactly. Say this, I have tried to talk to her, but she don't want nothin' to do with me since Carrie booted me out. Big Ol', that's Rex Loonsfoot, owns a garage in Hunter; I drive a wrecker for him on and off, says the way Kelly is ain't got nothin' to do with me bein' booted out. Says his three girls all treated him the same way, when they were that age. Says they're just understandin' what boys mostly want. Then, I guess they must get to thinkin' about how yer a boy too and maybe think how you been with girls too when you were younger and…and maybe just the idea of you bein' that way with their Mom, that's a tough thing to take for a girl. Hard to work out.

I remember when Big Ol' said that to me. It came into my head to think how would he know what it was like with a good happy family, 'cause he was in about the same shape as me when his girls were growin' up, so I says, "Yeah, but you weren't on good terms with Millie either then," I says. "So maybe it does have to do with me bein' on the outs with Carrie."

"Well, I was still in the house," Big Ol' says kinda humble like.

"Yeah, that's the loud house down the bend of the river, eh?" Chessy says and starts laughin'.

Chessy ain't never been married. Who the hell would marry him? He's built like a beer barrel with a face to match. Ah hell. I should talk. Anyway, it's easy for him to say, not bein' married. That was over at the River House, that talk, I think last Tuesday. May have been before that. My mistake was talkin' with Chessy there.

Time's funny when yer like me and ya don't work regular hours. I might have to work one place or another at 3 a.m., then get up at 6 a.m. and off to do some lawn work somewhere, or dry wall or windows, you never know. And out here at the lake? Well, not much to do but just caretake in the winter, but summer, them folks got all kinds of little projects. And sometimes they won't let ya leave till' yer done. They pay good though. Most of 'em. Except for the richest one of all, Old Man Chesterfield. The old man is the grandson of the first Chesterfield what was ever on the lake. He lets ya know that too. Don't know why that's supposed to be a big deal, but I guess it is. Lots of Hunter families have been here way longer than the Chesterfields. And, of course, The Tribe's been here a lot longer than the Chesterfields. Chipmunks and foxes and every bird in the trees too.

"Them Chesterfields didn't get rich by spendin' money on the here and there this and that," Pop says. "But at the end of the year they come through."

That's true enough. Usually comes in an envelope about

Dec. 15. Nice, healthy check. Both Pop and me get'em. There was a year or two there when my Christmas bonus kept food on the table for my kids. So, I can put up with a lot for that.

I look over at Kelly, and all I see is the back of her head and her pretty red hair. She's still lookin' out the window. Don't blame her. It's a nice view. Lot better than lookin' at her deadbeat old man.

I like this little church. Guess I said that. It's not a dark place like a lot of Catholic Churches, like the one down at the college in Hunter even. This one's got a lotta light in it. Lots of big windows and no colored glass. Clear. Clear. I keep figurin' Father Bill's gonna call for the colored glass comin' up here pretty soon. Catholics like their colored glass. 'Stained glass' I guess they call it. Funny name. Makes it sound like it's dirty or ruined somehow. Expensive, and I don't see the point really. I don't know, seems to me like you shouldn't have to dye God no colors. Seems like you shouldn't put nothin' between you and Him. I mean, lookin' out this window over Kelly's shoulder at the west end of the lake right now , seems like to me I can see Him clear enough. Wonder if that's what Kelly's lookin' out at now. I'd like to think we had that in common. But she maybe is just starin' at nothin' so's she don't have to look at me. That hurts a lot if it's true, but, like I say, I don't blame her. Or maybe she's just havin' some other thoughts. It don't have to be about me. Like to think whatever thoughts she's havin' are happy, but from the look on her face when she glances this way, I don't think they are.

Anyway, I've thought about how God seems to be right in these woods and on the lakes and rivers around here. I thought that lots of times out fishin' or huntin' back on the peninsula. Used to make a little bit a money guidin' back in there. But now the Lodge is closed down, don't expect there'll be much of that come fall. Never know though, maybe I can talk the board of the club into lettin' me go on guidin' even if there ain't no lodge guests. Guess I could do it anyway down on the river, but it ain't the same. I don't know them woods like I know these. Pop showed me every tree. Besides, don't wanna bust in on Shine and Chessy; they been doin' that for years. And they don't do much else. Good thing those two never got married. I don't feel better than many people, but I can't help but feel better than them. Should go to confession about that too, I guess.

I mean, how hard could it be to go to confession with Father Bill? He's a pretty level sort. Regular guy, you know? He ain't gonna make me feel like crap. He's even said to me, "Dale, we're all human. You and Carrie are going through a rough patch. Things work out if you let them. Especially for good people like you two."

That made me feel good. It made me feel like everybody in town don't think I'm a lowlife. The thing about Shine and Chessy that maybe makes me feel like I'm better than them, is that they don't think they got anything to be ashamed about. Them two are just proud of how much they can drink. And the other stuff they do. I don't ask. They don't tell, but I know there's some drugs involved. Did weed for a while, but all it did was make me hungry and sad. I told Chessy once, "I don't see no advantage to feelin' real happy for about an hour and then all sad and hungry and thinkin' hard and not very clear for the rest of the night."

Hughie says it gets to different people different ways. I guess that's right.

Huh, I remember this story Father Bill's readin'! Good Samaritan. Always liked this when I was little. The fella who everybody thinks is the lowlife ends up being the nicest to somebody hurt along the way. That's nice. That's nice. Makes me feel good some way. I try to be like that. When I pick up somebody with the wrecker, or when somebody I'm workin' for is havin' a bad day, I try to work quiet and even a time or two I give out some free advice, like Pop does sometimes. I ain't as good at is as Pop is though. And it ain't like anybody wants my advice. Not that anybody wants nobody else's advice, really…but maybe it helps sometimes…

Oh now, I like what Father Bill is sayin' about the story. "Who lies bleeding along your way? Who have you passed by?" Now if he just said that alone, that would make you feel guilty as hell, but then I like that he says, about the hitchhiker he didn't pick up once, and later ended up visiting the same kid at the hospital. He'd passed out along a winter road and almost froze to death. Easy to like Father Bill. He ain't one a those, "I'll-let-ya-know-when-yer-good-enough" priests. He sees us all walkin' along the same road. I like that.

Oh, oh, no money for the collection. Always hate when I forget. Mostly 'cause I know Ma's gonna put in double when she sees, then say, "Don't worry about it, honey." Makes me feel like a little kid. I know she don't mean it that way, but it's how I feel. If I'da bought one less round last night. But I didn't. And there it is I didn't. Until I get that fixed…until I get my head around Hughie, and Shine and Chessy, and stop bein' around'em for good, I ain't gonna be right with me, let alone Carrie and the kids. Hate feelin' like this, but I deserve it.

Ma don't know, that makes me feel like a little kid. Ain't her fault. And it gives Kelly one more reason to look out the window. I was her, I'd be lookin' out the window too, I guess. Nothin' I can do about it now, except try to remember next Sunday. Ah…who am I kiddin'?

Carrie's smarter than me. Course she went to college. Got the nursing degree. She does that hospice work. But she was way smarter even before she went to college. Seems like maybe folks go to college to get credit on paper for how smart they are. Course, how would I know? I'm proud of her. Don't think she knows how proud. I hope Kelly takes after her. Didn't start well, though with me gettin' her pregnant with our boy Isaac, "Ike" we call him, when we were just 16 and 15. He's 24 now, and I ain't got no idea where he is. Smart kid, took after Carrie, thank God. Carrie says that ain't true, that I can't see it, but Ike's just like me. "Same kind of brain." she says.

Well, Ike gets himself in trouble like I did. That's true. Got the Jessen girl pregnant when he was 18 and the two of them ran off. Doc Jessen, the girl's father, ain't heard from them either. Ike's friend Jason says he got a e-mail from them a year or two ago. They were out in California somewhere. I don't know whether to believe it. Jason's always been a liar and Ike never liked him much. Jason worked with Pop and me on a couple jobs last summer. Always had excuses for why he was late or didn't show up.

I don't think Carrie knows much more about it than I do. Not sure, though. Seems like she'd tell me, but maybe there's a reason she won't. So, I could have a grandchild somewhere, or not. Don't know what to make of that. If there was, it seems like Carrie would know it for certain. My boy Donny hardly remembers Ike. Don't know what Kelly remembers. Don't know Kelly, really. That makes me sad.

Well, here it is, The Our Father. Guess I daydreamed my way almost to the end of Mass. So maybe this'll be a good week. Now we kneel down for the 'I am not worthy'…huh, seems to fit right now… and off to Communion. Always like the wine with the bread. The mixin' there makes it feel special. Never liked wine much, except in church.

"The mass is ended. Go in peace."

One quick song and then here we are. Here we are.

"Dale, let's see what we can do about the grass and if we could spruce up the flower beds, oh and we're starting' to have some bat problems. Ha! Right in the belfry."

"Yes, Father."

"Oh you make that sound like you're in grade school."

He leans in close, "I wouldn't blame you if you told me to clean up my own bat shit!" Then he laughs and I just kinda sit there wide eyed and smilin'. You never know with Father Bill. You just never know.

"How about if you and I and Donny go fishing after supper? Then, maybe real late, just you and I can have a talk, without the liquor. And maybe about the liquor."

"Yes…"

He kinda eyes me up under them eyebrows, then winks.

I smile, "Well, we'll see about that after dinner. Ma said she's makin' her stuffed peppers to start."

"Now that sounds great. Gotta run down the road for 9 a.m. at St. Ann's. See you later."

"Bye Father."

Ma says, "You coming into Hunter for brunch, Dale?"

"Ah...I don't know...gotta mow the grass and look into the bats...out..."

Then I look at Donny lookin' at me. Kelly's already in the car. She slammed the door hard when I started sayin' I didn't know...

"Sure, sure Ma. Just let me get the truck."

"Okay. I'm cooking up some venison sausage."

"Well, can't pass that up!"

And then they're in the car and on the way down the gravel and Donny is lookin' out the window at me. I can see the... what...hope in his eyes. Carrie keeps his red hair cut short. When he was really little it just kinda hung in a mop. He was cute. Is cute. I'll say that even if he is my own kid. So I'm standing here thinking about all this when my danged cell phone goes off, and it's Big Ol' and some tourist down the river needs a wrecker, put his Lexus in ditch tryin' to drive inta Dr. Mayberry's camp. Bet there was some drinkin' involved there. Bet on it. Dr. Mayberry teaches science at the college. Likes the bottle. He's had The Puppies out for drinks there when some of his friends were up from Detroit and Chicago. Guess he does that all the time. I only went once though. Made me feel like we were on display for all them professors and rich fellas. Kinda like we were zoo animals. I ain't a mean sort, but that made me want to hit somebody. Got outta there.

Well, couple hours later I got some money back in my pocket from this friend of Mayberry's. Rides in with me, talkin' me up. Feelin' me out. Asks me all about life around here. What's the winters like, all that. I stayed friendly, but gave him lots of yups and nopes. Just enough funny bits to make him laugh. That's what he wanted. That's what I give him. Pop taught me that. This hind end coulda just rode along with Dr. Mayberry in the car behind all the way to the Fixall in Hunter, but no, he had to get him some local color. Well, I give it to him. Like Pop says, ya gotta make a livin'.

By the time I get over to Ma and Pop's, everybody is on their way for the day: Pop already at the church lookin' into the belfry probably. He shouldn't do that without me; he ain't gettin' any younger, but Ma told him what Father needed. Kelly's off with her friends somewhere. And then there's, Donny, who's waitin' for me. Ma has some sausage and eggs on the stove for me, and she sighs a time or two while she's makin' it. I tell her about the job I went out on. Didn't call her, knew she'd tell me to stop by and just pick up some food before I went. Knew I wouldn't get out of there right away, so, I just didn't call. Not right, I know. Don't know how else to handle it.

So I ask Donny if he wants to come along, help with the grass out at the church. He just grins. I got me a nice boy. I got me a nice boy. Got me another one somewhere. He's a nice boy too. Nice man I guess. Just got a pig head like me.

So we get back out to the church and Pop is just comin' down from the steeple.

"Pop, why did ya…"

He waves me off, "Lotta bat shit up there." He grins at me. "Good job for you and The Puppies."

I couldn't help laughing. Pop went kinda red in the face, when he saw that Donny heard him swearing, but then he laughed too. That started Donny laughing. It was nice, the three of us all having a laugh. I look at Donny kinda warnin' him not to tell his grandma that his grandpa cusses. Like she doesn't know already. He's a funny old coot. Big as me but even broader. Full beard mostly white now. I remember when it was fire red, like mine was when I grew it out for hunting season one year while I was still in my 20's. Carrie hated it. Said it made me look like a clown. I ain't grown it out since. Neither of them times seem so long ago. But they're gone any way you look at it. That's sure. Today, Pop was wearing his dirty overalls that Ma won't let in the house and an old Tigers hat he got when they won the World Series in 1984. Got it right at the stadium. Got me one too, but I lost it somewhere some drunk night. I guess I've lost a lot a things over the years.

"Pop," I say. "Did you scare all the bats away?"

"Oh, might have left one or two to bite you on the neck. Now don't take Donny up there, you know how they like little red haired boy's necks!" Then he winks at Donny. "I'll get this young jasper started on the grass. Then I'll take a look at the flower beds."

"Ah, Pop, me and Donny can…"

"Nope! I hear you and Donny got a appointment with Father to go fishin'! We gotta get the unimportant stuff out of the way."

My pop's a good sort. He come out of Vietnam and just kept on goin'. He was a grunt, too, right in the middle of it from what I can tell. Never says a word about it. Don't drink a drop of liquor. Don't hang out with a bunch of old drunks and talk about the war neither. But he don't take it out on me, just shoots me a look now and then that makes me know I'm outta line. Don't even do that all that often. All the crap I've pulled over my 40 years, and he's still right there with me. I don't know. I want to be more like him.

So Pop says, "There's a snow shovel already up there. I figure just throw her out the side and then we can scoop her up in a wheelbarrow later, maybe spread it on the flowers." Then him and Donny head out to take care of the yard, and I head for the steeple. It ain't very high. No more'n three and a half storeys or so. I'm up the ladder and near ankle deep in bat crap before I know it. Slugging away. That crack Pop made about me'n the Puppies doin' it together was just a joke. There ain't enough work there for all of us. Besides, he knows Shine and Chessy wouldn't stoop so low, and Big Ol' got his hands full at the Fixall, and Hughie, well Hughie just don't do any work. Too many bats floppin' around his head for that. Always got ideas, though, always. They always seem kinda innocent at first, just a way to have a fun night. Draws me right into'em. Ain't his fault though. What I do is my lookout. Pop taught me that at least. Maybe some day I'll get better at rememberin'. At 40 it's about time I guess.

Anyway, the bat crap is caked on pretty thick, but this is a good shovel and I got it flyin' out the side pretty quick. Have to keep duckin' my head to keep from hittin' it on the bell. Gotta remember where that ladder hole is too. That would be a fine way, right down to the floor. No sir. Gotta watch out for that.

Gonna have to get up here with some soap and water

too. Clean off the floor and the underside of the roof. Don't look forward to doin' that. Maybe save that for next Sunday. I take a shovelful and toss it out and I can see Donny going at the lawn like a regular workin' man and Pop crouchin' down weedin' out the flower garden. That makes me smile. Lookin' at Donny workin' away makes me think of Ike, and how hard it was to get him to do anything. One time, when he was about 10, I had him mowin' this same grass and I was up on a ladder fixin' some shingles and I spotted the little bugger dumpin' out the gas can back in the weeds by the parking lot, so he wouldn't have to mow much longer. Well, I came down that ladder awful fast. Handed him a five dollar bill and told him to take the gas can and walk the two miles down to the gas station out on the highway and fill that can back up, then bring it back. Told him the five I just give him was all the pay he was gettin' for that job.

He started to lie and I looked at him and he looked ashamed. And, well, he walked the can to the gas station, but I found it there full by the pumps when I took him back to get it in the truck later. Guess he filled it and then didn't want to face the walk back and me waitin' at the end. He didn't come back to the lake. Kept walkin' on towards Hunter, and Carrie spotted him. I don't know what he had in mind. Boys are funny. It's a long walk to Hunter from the highway.

Anyway, Carrie was bringing us out some lunch. She picked him up. He didn't say boo about what happened. Never said boo to me the rest of the day, except to tell me the can was at the station. She didn't press him for the full story. When I told her later, about how I sent him on a walk to refill the can, she just kinda looked me over. She says, "Now that was a little harsh, Dale."

Maybe it was. Maybe it was. Still seems like the boy got away with something to me. He did cut the grass later, though. And he never done it again. I don't suppose that made him over fond of me, though. I don't know.

Anyway, Pop and Donny make a nice picture down there. Nice sunny day, workin' away. Men workin' together. Nice view from here. Always like when you can look out over somethin', especially this lake. Makes you kinda glad inside. Sun comin' up off the water. Water just shimmerin', and five or six camps in clear view down the bay.

Camps, ha. Most of them ain't camps. Most of them make two of our little house in Hunter. Carrie's little house now, really, until I get my act together. It's been six months. Six months. For a while I was hopin' she'd give in, like she done before. But neither one of us is gettin' any younger, and I don't blame her any. Guess she'd just had enough. When I think about it, it's a miracle she ain't had enough a long time ago. She's the nearest I know to a saint.

"Whatcha doin', countin' the waves?"

I look down and Donny and Pop are standing next to each other lookin' up.

"'Bout done. Be right down."

Bit of a struggle comin' down the ladder with the shovel. Don't know how Pop managed getting it up there. He does lots of things at his age most guys don't. Nothin' seems to bug him one way or the other. I walk on out the back door of the church and Pop is just layin' in to shovel the bat crap into the wheelbarrow Donny rolled over.

'Bout then the phone rings.

It's Hughie, says he's got a bloody Mary waitin' for me out to the River House, and says we got some stuff to talk out. We don't usually drink bloody Marys, but I guess he figures that's a way to get me to come out...somethin' special like.

Well, we do have some stuff to talk out. I gotta figure a way to tell him I ain't goin' out drinkin' with him no more. Figure he probably got Marcie Sheldrake to push his tab for the one drink, or maybe he even promised Marcie that I'd pay, since by now Hughie's talked to Big Ol' and he knows I got some money in my pocket. One thing will lead to another sure as short hairs and we'll end up out to somebody's camp or back down the hill in the boathouse drunk as skunks. Won't say I ain't tempted, but it's Sunday; not like that ain't happened on Sunday before, but today seems different and Pop and Donny eyein' me up helps me feel stronger that way. And Father talkin' about fishin' tonight and talkin' with me about the bottle, and I get the feelin' we'll be talking about another subject later on, maybe my gettin' back with Carrie... And, well, it just ain't gonna happen, at least not today...I hope. One day at a time, I guess.

"No...no Hughie, I got stuff I gotta get done. Got my boy and it's Sunday; you'll have to go without me."

Wanted to tell him, 'go on without me now and every day from now on'; couldn't bring myself to say it. Might be a lie in the long haul and that'd break Donny's heart...again...if I went back on it.

"Oh come on, ya pussy! When has Sunday ever stopped ya? I'm buyin'. Maybe meet Chessy and Shine later out to Mayberry's camp. Doc Mayberry probably be grateful. Heard you bailed his pal out earlier."

"No. I'm not comin' today, Hughie." I wanted to add to that, 'What if Mayberry is grateful to me? Why should you get the profit of it?' But I didn't want to wrangle him any more. I just wanted to be rid of him.

"Ah, you'll change your mind. You know ya will. Why ya flappin' your gums about all that Sunday shit when you know you're gonna end up with the Pups? Just kiddin' yourself."

"Maybe, maybe, Hughie. But that's my business."

"Oh...ha...'my business'. Okay, see ya in about a hour Mr. 'my business'."

That kinda ticked me off.

"Well, wait if ya want, Hughie. I ain't comin'."

"Bye Padre. Just remember I know who you are. I know where you really live."

I wanted to say "Fuckya very much!" and hang up, but the boy was right there so I says, "Bye Hughie."

Pop kinda gives me a real pleased look. Grins, then says, "Puppy trouble?"

He didn't have to say that, that was grindin' it a little, but I guess he can't resist. Can't blame him really. I've had 'puppy trouble' for 19 years and more.

Got kinda proud then and said somethin' maybe I

shouldn't'a. "Well, there ain't gonna be no puppy troubles any more." I gave him kind of a stiff jaw look.

Then I look over and I see Donny just takin' it in, believin' what his old man says 100 percent. I almost cry. How can I let him down again?

"Okay, okay, that sounds good." Pop says, just lettin' that flow by. "Let's get this guano on the flowers."

"What's 'guano' Poppie?"

"Oh, don't you know? Little boys are just full of it," Pop says.

That snaps my bad mood and I start in to shoveling up what I dropped from the steeple, pretty good pile. I keep on laughin' for a while after.

Donny keeps lookin' at me and Pop and sayin', "What?" while he helps to shovel with the little spade. Then Pop wheels the first load ten feet over to the flower garden and we spread it out there and go back for more. This goes on for better part of an hour, but I never quite stop laughin'. Pop is funny, don't even have to try.

Now, Hughie thinks he's funny. Always got jokes, most of'em filthy. I'll admit I've laughed at'em a time or two…well…hell…most of the time, who am I kidding'? But Pop doesn't have to try. He's a smart old man. Ma and Carrie say I'm smart too, but I don't see it. Seems like most of the smart went out of me when I went to Afghanistan with the National Guards in 2012.

Nineteen years ago I was all over with the Marines, never got close to the action really. Worked as a cook, mostly on bases. That was fine with me. I signed up with the guards after my Marine reserve time was up, just to make some easy money on weekends. Carrie didn't want me to, but we needed money. But then in 2012, when I'm goin' on towards 40 years old, all of a sudden us weekenders get called up to stand in for a Marine unit that's got delayed on their way to Afghanistan, and 72 hours after leavin' here I'm rollin' down a desert road and we hear there's a ambush up ahead, then a roadside bomb goes off hits the Bradley right in front of us and next thing I know I'm with the medic tendin' to some poor fella, a kid really, right outta high school, Bruce Crandall was his name, from over in the Sault, just screamin', no words, just screamin', with his legs blowed off at the side of the road. Can't never get that out of my head once I start thinkin' about it.

Well, Crandall didn't make it. After that, I don't think I'm so smart anymore. I don't think I know much. 'Cause I don't understand what happened over in that desert that day or any other day, that's for sure. Just wanted to come home as soon as I could. See Carrie, the kids. Wanted to hug Ike. Wanted to at least find out where he was. Somehow I didn't do any of that. Just fell back in with the Puppies.

Thought about to bringin' it all up with Pop a time or two, but he never bothered nobody with what he saw in Vietnam. Didn't think it was fair. And then I got real down, got so even the Pups wouldn't hang with me. Found myself out on a river bank some mornings. Time or two I didn't know where the truck was. Last time was six months ago. When I got home, Carrie said not to bother comin' in. She had a bag packed for me, said I'd have to live elsewhere. I didn't get mad. Not my way really. I give myself credit for that. I ain't a mean drunk. Didn't blame her at all, really. Been tryin' to get better. Last night was a slip back. Now Hughie wants me to go off again. I ain't gonna do her. Anyway, I don't wanna talk about the bomb on the road and poor Bruce Crandall, like I always do when I get drunk. I'm hopin' maybe I can put the Puppy stuff behind me too; maybe this with Hughie is a first step. First step. I don't know. Gonna be tough.

So we finish up there at the church and I promise Donny I'll go throw a baseball with him down at the field in Hunter. I managed to make most of his games this summer. It gettin' on into August, that's over now, but he likes to play. Me, I wasn't never very good. Could hit, and play the field, but I never seemed to care about it the way the other kids did. Just wanted to run in the woods, go fishin'. Don't know. I guess there's a couple different kinds a fellas. I ain't the court and ballfield kind really. But I like throwin' a baseball with Donny.

So, I promise I'll do'er. Donny and Pop head off in Pop's new Ford to get our baseball gloves and I put the shovels and such away. I'm feelin' pretty good about the whole thing. I close everything down and look her over and it all looks clear and nice. And I head on over to the parking lot. It's a good day. So I'm rollin' in the old truck down to Hunter and the phone rings again.

"Hughie, I told ya I ain't comin' and I ain't."

"C'mon Padre, one drink."   ·

"One drink like last night? I ended up in the boathouse, Hughie. I ain't doin' it. What's more I think maybe you and me better have a talk right now…"

"This about how you're goin' back to Carrie and leavin' the Pups behind."

"Well, I wouldn'ta put it that way, but maybe I gotta."

"Do you know how many times…"

"Yeah I do. This time I mean it."

"…Where ya headed?…"

"Down to play catch with my boy."

"I'll bring my glove. We'll have a catch and then take the kid along with us. I'll give him some pointers."

"No you won't. You ain't comin'. Not if yer my friend."

"Hey, I ain't the one talkin' about leavin' the Pups behind."

"No, that's me. And I want ya ta pay attention to that idea, Hughie, 'cause it's real."

"You know, you woke up in the boathouse. Ha, I woke up in Chesterfield's front room. Nobody was up though."

"Don't know whether that's a lie or not, either way you're on your own, Hughie. I ain't vouchin' for ya any more. And quit tryin' to change the subject."

"Tough talk for an old friend."

"Hughie don't do that."

"How long we known each other…"

"Hughie, I'm hanging' up. Take care of yourself."

This is gonna be tough. This is gonna be the toughest thing ever. Like it or not Hughie is gonna go hunt up Chessy and Shine and they're all gonna show up at the ball park. Well, let'm. And maybe it's good Donny hears what I'll say too. I'll just be nice.

It's good to show a kid that you can say no in a nice way. Maybe gives 'em an idea about havin' character like Miss Antilla used to tell us when I took that home-ec class in high school. All the Puppies was laughin' at me for bein' in there, but Carrie was in there and I knew a good thing when I seen it. Still the best thing in my life. Worth losin' a few friends over. Gotta keep tellin' myself that. They ain't really my friends if I lose 'em. I'll feel bad about Hughie. Him and me been friends since kindergarten and when he helped me with my bloody nose second day a school that year on the playground. Missy Goetz gave it to me. She was a big girl. Even in high school. In kindergarten she was a giant. Ol' Hughie helped me out that time. But I've more than paid him back. Bail money four times I think. One time had to borrow it from Pop. Service didn't seem to touch Hughie at all. 'Course with his old man he was pretty screwed up before he went. He was never in the thick of it. He was out on one a them aircraft carriers in the gulf. Said it was like livin' in a floatin' city. Said only real danger was goin' stir crazy in your bunk. He was a good mechanic. Worked for Big Ol' for a while, but Big Ol' Rex—we called him BOR for a while when we were in high school—he finally had enough and told Hughie to stay away from the Fixall. That was after he took the money from the till. I don't blame Big Ol' one bit. Big Ol' was a heck of a football player. I ain't much of a fan, but I remember seein' him toss guys around that field. I've seen him toss more than one guy in a fight too. But we're all gettin' older. Big Ol' goes close to 300 now and his knees are bad.

So I drive down the Hunter road past Porcupine Rise off to the east and roll down the hill into Hunter and pull in by the ballfield. Donny's already there with the baseball gloves. I can't help smilin'. Off to the north I can see the college buildings and St. Ann's up on College Hill.

I get outta the truck, slam the door and Donny comes runnin' over just beamin'.

"Ya ready?" I say.

He don't say nothin', just keeps smilin'. What a nice little boy.

I go and crouch down behind the plate and he goes out to the mound. He was a fair pitcher in his league. Second best on the team I'd say. Doesn't throw that hard, but he throws strikes. At that level, that's all that matters. Just get'em across.

Well, we been at it for ten minutes or so now and sure enough here comes Shine's old Chevy and Chessy and Shine and Hughie pile out. All with baseball gloves. Can't imagine where they found'em.

Hughie says, "How old ya gotta be to join this league?"

Donny's face kinda falls and I say under my breath, "Don't worry, chum, they're leavin'."

"Afraid you're over the age limit fellas."

"Nah," Hughie says, "I ain't much more'n forty and these two ain't even that old, right Donny?"

Donny, bein' the nice little fella he is just smiles, but it's sick around the edges.

I kinda cross my arms, "Private catch fellas. Just me and my boy."

Chessy and Shine kinda look at Hughie. Neither one a them has the sense God gave a carrot and they've been bad news since we were in seventh grade, just lookin' for somethin' to drink or smoke and swallow and stick in their arms. I don't hardly remember what they were like before that. Seems like they were nice little guys like Donny, didn't say much, that's what worries me. They're just takin' their lead from Hughie, like always. They even both went into the Navy with Hughie, but neither one made it through basic. They were both back after two weeks.

"The Puppies are breakin' up," Hughie says. "That's what the Padre tells me over the phone. What ya think of that, Shine?"

Chessy steps over to Hughie. "Maybe, let's go on out to Mayberry's. Dale's busy here."

"Ya, Padre's busy, Chess. Too busy for his old friends."

"Ya don't gotta make it like that, Hughie." I says, but you know, I'm really kinda glad when Shine and Chessy start headin' for the car.

"Maybe I'll just stay here and watch Dale have his catch,"

Hughie says.

"Suit yourself," I say. I look over at Donny. "Let's see your fast ones."

Donny just beams and goes back out to the mound. Hughie sits down on the bench by the backstop and watches for a while. Shine guns the engine a time or two. Hughie sees I ain't waverin', feels dumb I guess and gets up.

"This ain't over," he says to me.

"Yeah, it is, Hughie." I say. "Pay attention to what I'm tellin' ya."

"You'll change your mind."

"We'll see."

"Yeah, we will," he says as he's gettin' in the car. "You ain't no better 'n us."

They pull away.

Donny watches'em go. Looks at me and says, "Yeah you are, Pop."

I nod just to hold the tears back. This's been a long time comin'. I hope it really has come for this little boy's sake. I gotta make it so it has. Gotta remember the proud look on his face. Gotta remember, that even after all I put him and his sister and his mom through, he's still proud'a me.

So we do the pitch and catch a while longer and all of a sudden I look up on this clear blue summer day and here comes Carrie with a bag and a thermos and a couple of plastic cups. Prettiest thing I seen in a while, her with her short dark hair. Strong little woman, 'compact' I think she calls herself, with the nicest smile. That, that strength, that's what got me first about her, no matter what Hughie and the Puppies say. She sets the thermos and stuff down on the bench along the first base line and turns to go.

"Where ya off to?" I say.

"Just brought you boys a little snack."

"You shoulda saw Pop, Ma."

"Should have seen…" she says.

I grin a little bit. She always does that to me too.

"Huh?"

"The right way is 'should have seen'."

"Right how?"

"Never mind. What should I have seen your Dad do?"

"Donny…" I say. She don't need to know 'till it's real for sure.

"Hughie and them other Puppies showed up, and Pop just sent'em away again. Said there ain't gonna be no more shenanigans."

"How does your grandpa talk through your mouth? 'Shenanigans'…'" Carrie says, her dark hair shinin' in the sun. She looks over at me and I kinda melt…just like always. She's smilin' at me for the first time in a good while. I smile back. She turns, says over her shoulder, "I hope that's true Donny."

"I seen it."

"Saw it."

"Huh?"

I laugh, she waves without looking back. Carrie ain't takin' nothin' for granted and I don't blame her.

"Let's see what your ma brung us."

"Brought us," he says and grins at me, the little scamp.

I reach over and grab his hair and pull it kinda playful like. He laughs, then I tickle him and he starts laughing so hard it makes me laugh too. Well, that's the best I've felt about things in a while: that moment right there.

Chocolate chips and milk never stop bein' good no matter how old you get. I think when ya go out on benders night after night you start losin' track of how good just a regular day can be, how good just little things can be. When I look at the rest of the Puppies, I kinda feel bad. Oh, Shine was married once for a little right outa high school, but that wasn't never gonna last. Chessy ain't never been married. If he ever is, unless he changes an awful lot and starts cuttin' his hair more than once a year and bathin', that ain't gonna happen either. Only Big Ol' and me got wives and kids. His are mostly growed up now. He had'em young then got himself fixed. That was Milly's idea. It ain't a bad one. Those two go at it some, and Big Ol' has it comin' for hangin' around with Hughie and me and sometimes even them other two. I don't know what's gonna happen now. Last time I was straight with Carrie, Hughie went off the deep end. I told Carrie I had ta help him.

"We been friends since kindergarten!" I tried to explain to her.

"Yeah," she says, "well we've got kids together, Dale. I think that's more important."

That time I kinda waved her off and went to help him, ended up not helpin' myself. Ended up outa my own house for good reason: bein' a jackass, like Pop would put it.

Well, if I can help it, and I think I can this time; I'm done with that.

About then two things happen: the phone rings again, another call from the Fixall, busy Sunday, and Lester, our old mix breed, shows up to get Donny. Musta got out when Carrie went in. He's a funny lookin' dog, like a lab in the ears, but with whiskers like one'a them scotty dogs and a long nose like a collie.

Pop said he wouldn't win at a dog show for "Best of Breed" but he would for "Most of Breed". Pop's pretty funny.

Anyway Lester shows up, just waggin' his tail. Call is just a flat on some old tourist lady's car 10 miles towards the Soo, that's what we call Sault Ste. Marie around here. Twenty minute job. No reason Donny and Lester can't go along for the ride, so I hand Donny the phone and he calls his Ma. It's all square, so we head out.

After we go over to the Fixall and pick up the wrecker, and head on our way, Donny asks me when I'm comin' back home.

I get brave, only regret it a little, and say, "Maybe pretty soon."

He smiles, kinda nods, pets Lester, looks out the window. Then he says, "Do you talk to Ike?"

That kinda shakes me up. Didn't see it comin'. "No," I say. "I ain't heard from your brother in a long time."

"Ma does," he says and then looks at me. "Don't tell I told."

I shake my head. Surprises me a little, but actually makes me feel better. Least I know he's still alive, though I don't know where he is. Wonder if Carrie knows where he is, or if he just calls nonymous. Anyway, if he's gonna talk to somebody in the family, probably good it's Carrie. I just piss him off mostly. Don't even try to. Just happens. I dunno.

Comin' up the hill I see Kelly walkin' along with one of her girlfriends. Julie…Swanberg, think that's her name. Nice kid. Her dad's a math teacher at the college, just came to town this year. I did some work over to her house on the plumbing. I roll down the window. If Kelly's with her friend, maybe she'll talk to me.

"Hi girls," I say. "Headin' out on a call. Gotta fix a old lady's tire. Just down the road. Wanna pile in? Maybe stop for ice cream after?"

Julie kinda looks at Kelly, and Kelly says, "No, thanks, Dad." Then she kinda smiles sly like. "But maybe you could give us money for ice cream?"

"Tell ya what," I say.

And I notice Kelly kinda takes a deep breath, afraid I'm gonna say somethin' dumb I guess. She's got her reasons.

"When we get back from the call I'll meet ya over to the Dairy Isle, and I'll buy ya whatever ya want, sound good?"

Kelly kinda smiles, looks a little surprised and says, "Sure, Dad. Um…you'll be there, right at Frozen Delights?"

That kinda stings a little, but I say, "Count on it."

Her face kinda wrinkles up, but she manages another smile, pullin' her long red hair out of her eyes in the wind. I guess that was the wrong words. She's heard that before.

I kinda swallow, smile, and just say, "See ya there. Promise. 'Bout a hour."

"Okay."

"Bye, Mr. Sylvanus." Julie says. Like I said, nice kid. Good manners.

"See ya soon girls," I say and roll up the window.

★★★

The old tourist lady is a pill. She's short and pretty gray and a little hunched over. She's got on a fancy hat and she's on her way somewhere. She gets out of her car and kinda stomps towards me right there along M-28.

"What took you so long?"

"Got here quick as I could M'am."

"With a dog and a boy in the truck?"

"That's my son and his dog, M'am."

"Well, why are we standing here? Fix my tire!"

"Right away M'am."

I go for the jack and she keeps jabberin' away at me. Tells me I ain't gettin' no tip. I don't say what I wanta say which would be, "You can stick your tip, you old sourpuss." I just say, "We'll be done in a few moments, M'am."

And we are and I'm back on the way to the Dairy Isle.

"How come that lady was so mean to you, Pop?"

"Oh her? She wasn't mean. She's just old. Sometimes, for some old ladies, and men too really, bein' old and cranky is the only thing that keeps 'em happy."

"That's weird."

"Yup, but it's true. I seen it all the time. They're maybe shut up in a house alone. Maybe their husband died a long time ago and they ain't got nobody to pick on anymore, or really just to talk to, so they take it out on everybody else they meet."

"That's weird."

"Yup, but like I say. It's true."

As we go around the corner towards Hunter I can see him thinkin' it over. Lots to learn. Lots to learn. Hope he learns it better'n' me. Doesn't have to go half around the world, half around the bend just to come back to his own home and family to finally get it right. Hope that's where I've got to now. I dunno.

At the Dairy Isle Kelly and her friend Julie are waiting for us.

"Hi, Daddy," Kelly says when I get out of the truck. I give the kids some cash and they go up and order on their own. I get a strawberry malt. Haven't had one in a long time. We all sit down at a picnic table around on the west side of the stand.

"Nothing like a Dairy Isle," I say to nobody and everybody. This is a good day.

Kelly laughs, "A Dairy what?"

I look at her smilin' just in general, but I don't know what she's laughin' at. Then I figure it out.

"Ain't it the Dairy Isle?"

"We tell you this every time! It's 'Frozen Delights', Pop," Donny says grinning around his ice cream.

"Well, it'll always be 'Dairy Isle' to me," I say. "That's what it was when I was a kid."

"That was during the Civil War, right?" Kelly says.

And I almost cry. My little girl is jokin' with me like we used to when she was little. Maybe she doesn't hate me quite so much as I thought. What a good day!

"C'mon, I'm not that old…"

"Don't worry, Pop," Donny says, not even cracking a smile, "I won't let Kelly put you in a home."

Julie kinda lets out a little breath, while my kids laugh and says, "You guys are so mean! You're Dad's not old at all!"

"You've got a crush on my Dad!" Kelly says and pokes her then runs off.

"I do not!" Julie says and chases after her.

Kelly yells over her shoulder, "See you at supper, Dad! You'll be there…right?"

"Lord willin' and the creek don't rise! Gotta be, Father Bill is comin'."

"Thanks, Mr. Sylvanus!" Julie says.

"See, you do like him!" Kelly says and they disappear down the block and around the corner towards the south campus below college hill.

Donny and I sit and talk at the…well…whatever it's called now, for another half hour. We talk about his baseball season and about school. I tell him how important it is.

"It's boring, Pop."

"Well, guess I always felt that way too, but you pay attention. You don't want to end up like me, Donny."

"Why not? I think you do pretty good."

"Well, thanks, chum, but don't ya want to be smart like your Mom? Go to college?"

"I don't know."

"Well, if you do, you get a lot more chances than what I got. I went into the service, and that was okay, but I think college would be better for you."

"How come?"

"Well…well it just would see?"

"Unh unh."

I laugh. Truth is I don't know nothin' about college really other than where it is and that some smart folks work there and graduate from there.

"Well, maybe you better talk to your Ma about it. She went there."

"Oh she talks about it all the time."

"Then how come yer askin' me?"

"You brought it up."

I kinda toss his hair and laugh.

"Okay," I say. "See you're already smarter than me. You go to college, promise?"

"Okay."

Next we head over to the Fixall to drop off the truck. Light's on in the garage so I stick my head in there. Big Ol' is elbow deep in his jeep engine. The jeep's covered with mud.

"Break down?"

He doesn't look up, "Nope, but I was about to. Carburetor."

"Need a hand?"

He looks up wipes away some grease with his hand and puts more grease there accidental-like, reaches for a rag.

"Hey Donny!"

"Hello Mr. Callaghan."

"Big Ol', is fine," he says grinning at Donny.

Donny looks up at me, "Pop and Ma says it ain't."

Big Ol' laughs. "Why don't you go out front and grab a candy bar off the rack, Donny? Yer dad'll be right out."

"For free?" His eyes get big.

"If ya hurry," Big Ol' says.

Donny runs out.

"What's this I hear?" Big Ol' says when he's gone.

"Now don't start…"

"No, I think it's good." He reaches back into the engine. I grab him a wrench before he asks for it.

"What are we talkin' about, just to be sure?"

"You and Hughie and Chessy and Shine. Hughie came in here with a full head of steam twenty minutes ago. Said yer gettin' your nose up in the air. Too good for him."

"I never said…"

Big Ol' puts up his hand, "Ya are too good for'em. To be honest, I was gettin' worried about ya."

"Now you just worry about yerself, Rex. I'll take care…"

"Shut up for a minute. Ever since you came back, when was it 2012?"

I look away, nod.

"Ever since ya got back, ya been worse than ever. I can't keep up with ya and I'm three times yer size."

"Twice," I say and smile at him.

He laughs. "I'm serious, Dale. Good for you. Them guys are no good, never have been. We both know that."

"Well, I don't think I'm so different."

"Ya are though. We both are. Now don't go tryin' to make it look good for'em. They don't stop pretty soon the clock's gonna run out on all three of'em. I was worried the same thing was gonna happen to you." He wipes some sweat off his forehead. Nobody sweats like Big Ol'. I worry about the way he sucks in air sometimes when he gets warm too. That heart's havin' a bad time keepin' the blood movin' around that big old body. That's what Carrie says anyway. After a minute he says, "Carrie know what happened today?"

"Well…yeah…Donny told her right after it happened."

"Well, that's just fine, Dale. Really it is."

I nod again. This ain't exactly our usual talk.

"So, where was ya muddin'?"

"Oh, down the river. Usual places. That's got it!" He says and closes the hood. "Now get on outta here. Any luck I won't be callin' ya out again today. Sunday night, should be quiet."

"If ya don't mind, maybe you could take any calls come later? I'm supposed to have supper with Father Bill. Then we're havin' a talk."

"Uh oh. Sounds like he's gonna give ya a 'come to Jesus'."

"Well, I guess I could do worse."

"Ya, and ya have. So have I. That'll be fine, Dale. Catch ya on the flip flop."

"Thanks, Rex."

He grins, "Like I told yer boy, it's 'Big Ol'."

"Nope," I say. "Today, you were, Rex. I appreciate it."

"Nothin' to appreciate. You done the same for me. More times-n-I can count."

"Let's hope I can stick to it. Stayin' off the sauce. Keepin' it all straight."

"Well, I'll do my best to keep Hughie outta your face."

"Thanks, Rex. I appreciate that." I smile at him and it's kinda uneasy for a second.

Finally he says, "Later."

I head on out and Donny is waitin' in my truck with his candy bar.

"Another couple days like this and your teeth will fall out. Don't let yer ma see that candy bar."

He jams the whole thing in his mouth.

"What candy bar?" he says with his mouth full.

I laugh pretty hard, shake my head and start up the truck.

At dinner, Father Bill is looking at me funny. So is Ma, when she sits down at the table to eat. She don't usually do that much, keeps going back and forth to the kitchen mostly. Pop is just looking at me like he always does. He's pretty steady that way. Don't get worked up about much a nothin'. Donny is like always: this time trying to see how many pork chops he can eat. Kelly eats like a bird. I half hoped Carrie might show up, but Ma says she has the late shift, won't show up to get the kids till tomorrow morning. Kids might just walk over there. She might not come at all. That makes me a little sad, but I can see why she ain't rushin' over to see me. She don't wanna get her hopes up, I guess. I can't blame her for that at all.

Father Bill is still lookin' at me. Eyein' me up like something is new. Doesn't seem like he's mad or disappointed. Just looks like he's tryin' to figure somethin'. Do I look different? I do feel a little different, just in these last 12 hours or so. Funny how that happens. Hope it lasts.

"Another stuffed pepper, Father?" Ma's bringin' a whole new tray of 'em in. We already had the pork chops and potatoes. "Just to fill in the corners?" She's grinnin' wide. She likes havin' Father Bill over. She likes Father Bill. Who don't? Likable guy.

"Oh Betty," Father Bill says, "I suppose I must. And he smiles up at her and digs into his third stuffed pepper.

They are awful good, but I hold off 'cause I know there's some blueberry pie comin'. Probably with ice cream. I look over at Donny, hope he don't make himself sick.

"Easy there, son," I say.

He grins. "I'm good. I can eat lots more."

Pop says, "Much more you'll turn into a pork chop."

Donny almost spits out his food. Nothin' much funnier than picturing a walkin' talkin' pork chop to a kid his age, unless it's somethin' about poop. That's the real killer. I still remember how funny that was for me. Words are funny. And "poop" to a ten-year-old? Well, that's just the topper.

"Can I come out to the lake with you tonight, Daddy?" Kelly says.

That shakes me up a bit. "You wanna go fishin' with us?"

"Well," she says. "No. I just thought maybe Julie and me could go swimming at the lodge while you're out; then maybe build a fire in the fire pit?"

"Why...sure..."

"She just wants to go meet that kid." Donny says. Pesky look on his face.

"What kid?"

"That, Henry Chesterfield..."

"Donald, you mind your business!" Ma has just walked in with the pie and gives Donny a serious look.

"Okay, gram."

"Well, Dad, can I?" Kelly says. Looks like there's been arrangements made. I can't think of a reason to say no. Wish Carrie was here, though.

"Sure, honey. That'll be fine."

Pop gives me a wink. Father just smiles and finishes his pepper.

★★★

When we get back to the lodge at Hunter Lake from our fishing trip, about four hours later, it's comin' up on 9 o'clock. Donny caught a couple undersize perch, Father caught a little bass that made him happy, and I pulled in a pike that'll be good for a supper comin' up. 40 inches. Not bad. Donny got all excited when I let him net the pike. He's still jabbering away as I step out to pull the boat in. I drop the bass and the pike into the live trap off the little dock by shore. Father says he'll clean 'em in the morning. That really means I will, and we both know it, but I don't care much. Father says 'hi' to Henry. None of us were very surprised when he was waiting for Kelly by the lodge when we first got here, the Chesterfield's bein' just down the bay from the lodge and St. Brigid's, and asks the girls what they been up to. They're both too red in the face to say boo, so he says, "Well, Henry what have these girls been up to?"

Henry turns red too, "Well, we've just been making the fire, Father."

"And a good fire it is, Henry. Guess I'll get up to the church and wash up a bit. Could you come pick me up on your way out, Dale?"

"Well, I guess I will, Father." I smile at him feeling as easy as I have in a very long time. "Wouldn't do for our priest to walk back to Hunter."

"Well, even if something bad happened, some good Samaritan would come along." He winks at me, pulls the few strands of hair he's got back over his bald head.

I laugh at that. The kids don't because they weren't listening this morning. Funny but that makes me feel good. Reminds me of all the times when I was little that big folks were talkin' about somethin' I didn't understand.

Father heads up the hill and before I get the boat pulled all the way up, usin' a log as a roller, the kids are all in the woods playin' at somethin'. I just sit and watch the fire a while. I hear a car out on the road and I hope it ain't Hughie comin' to look for me. That would ruin this good day. Funny thing is, there's a part of me kinda wants him to come. Some part'a me wants to disappear from all this goodness. Why? I don't understand it myself.

This day seems like the first day in a long while, when I really felt in control. Haven't thought about the war or that fella screamin' by the side of the desert road much. Haven't thought about goin' and gettin' a fifth and pourin' it down. Haven't even thought about a beer. Just had me a real good day.

Fire is startin' to burn down. Wasn't much of a fire to begin with. Mostly sticks. Henry ain't no boy scout. Seems like a nice boy, though. Wonder which one of the girls he's got a crush on. I can't tell if Kelly is the one with the crush on him or if she set this up for Julie. Never could read girls good. Donny's got a little boy crush on Julie, though. That's for sure. He don't even know it. I do know a thing or two about little boys that way.

"Kids," I call out into the half dark. "I'm goin' up to talk to Father for a bit. Then we'll be down to head home. Maybe a hour."

I don't hear nothin' from the woods.

"Hear me?" I call out real friendly.

"Yes, Dad," Kelly calls back, kinda sarcastical, but I don't mind much.

"Okay, then."

I start up the hill.

The loons are calling out on the lake. Hard not to like that sound. They're somethin', them birds. I know Doc O'Brian, the English professor, who has a place out here I done some work on, really likes to watch'em. He told me all about'em once. Said they live to be over 50 years old. You wouldn't think it, but I believe him. He's lived out here all his life. Don't know how he come to know all that. Maybe just from watchin'em and readin' about'em.

He's a poet, not no scientist, but he spends a lot of time out on the lake winter and summer. I've know'd him since I was a kid. He was my high school teacher before he went over to the college. I don't know if that's a promotion or how that works, really.

When I get into the church Father Bill is up near the front prayin'. I can tell 'cause he's on his knees. I don't know whether to go on or no.

Without turnin' around he says, "All finished up with the Big Guy, Dale. C'mon up."

I walk up kinda uneasy, never know what Father Bill's got up his sleeve. He looks at me when I sit down and kinda smiles. It's funny. He never asks if I want to go to confession, never forces anybody to pray with him. Never even just starts in to pray assuming everybody else will. He waits to be asked to do anything. He told me once when I first met him, and I musta looked a little put off by him bein' a priest, "I'm just a man, Dale. Not even always all that good a man." Then he grinned at me. That's the way he was lookin' at me now in that half light in the church. I could see he had a question.

"You had a good day today, didn't you Dale?" he says.

"Well…yeah."

"It's all over your face. Would you tell me about it?"

So I start in talkin' about the day, not even leavin' out how it started in the boathouse with a hangover after another bad night with Hughie. I trust him, besides Hunter's pretty small and since it's his business, I figured he knowed already. He even kinda nodded like he was sayin', 'Yeah, I know that part'. Anyway, I tell him about what I was thinkin' in church and about how much I like the Samaritan story, and about Donny and Kelly, and finally I get around to my dust up with Hughie and the Puppies, about the old lady with the flat, about seein' Carrie at the ball park.

"That must have been pretty hard to face those guys down like that, Hughie and the others."

"Well, my boy was there. I almost had to."

Father Bill laughs, looks away, looks back. "Still, I know that was always hard for me: saying no to my old drinking buddies."

I kinda look at him like I don't get it.

"I'm a recovering alcoholic, Dale."

"Oh...I didn't know."

"Well, I don't make it a secret, but it doesn't always come up in conversation. Thirty years, sober."

"Wow, well I didn't know."

"You can come and talk to me any time, just like this, Dale. I can take you to meetings too, if you want."

"Well...I don't know, Father. Truth is...and I know yer gonna say that all drunks...whoops I mean..."

"'Drunks' is fine, no need to pretend."

"Well, all drunks probably say they're not drunks, but I ain't sure I'm one. See, I don't have a problem not drinking. Always have been able to just stop. What I miss is headin' out with the Puppies, that's what we call ourselves, havin' some wild times, jokes, huntin', fishin' muddin' trips, like that. Especially when I start thinkin' about... or dreamin' about what I seen in the war...especially this one time..."

"Go on."

So, I tell him about the fella by the side of the road in Afghanistan.

"You need some company then? Somebody to talk to, when that comes into your head?"

"Ya, and the drinkin' seems to go with that..."

"Yes. Yes it does. Well, if the drinking isn't the biggest something you have to beat, you're lucky. That's my biggest cross."

"Huh?"

"Hardest thing I have to deal with, my burden, like Jesus carrying the cross."

"Oh, I get ya. That bad, huh?"

He nods, gives me kind of a sad little smile, "Some days." He shakes me up, the way he's so real and...well...just like anybody.

"Dale, why don't you talk to Carrie about...those things?" he asks after a minute.

"Oh, Father, I can't do that. That ain't right. She's got enough to worry about with the kids and what she does with all them dyin' people. Besides, I don't wanna make her feel bad for me."

"Okay. Fair enough. I'll make you a deal. Next time you feel like you want to go out with 'The Puppies' you call me, huh?"

"Really?"

"Yeah. I like to hunt and fish, but I'm not real big on 'wild times'. Still, it might just be a way to stay straight with your kids, maybe even Carrie." He puts out his hand. I take it.

"I hope I don't let you down, Father. That would make me feel bad."

"I'm more worried about you letting yourself down, Dale." And he looks at me real serious like. His eyes kinda tied right up in mine for a second. I'll do all I can to help you. You know, it's funny, I'd been planning to have this talk with you for a while. I even set up this fishing trip just so we could do it. And then you go and take matters into your own hands and start towards the straight and narrow all on your own. The Lord works in mysterious ways. Makes my job easier, if I just trust."

"I guess so."

"You know what else? Your mother took me aside right after dinner and asked me to have a talk with you."

"Ha…Ma."

"From the way your Dad was looking at me, I think he had a hand in it too."

"Pop. He's a funny old bird. Never know what's goin' on with him. He'll surprise ya."

"People do that."

"Father…"

"Yeah?"

"I got kind of a funny question for ya…

"If you're a alcoholic, how do you drink the wine in church?"

"It's mustum."

"Huh?"

"A kind of wine that has fermentation, but no alcohol."

"Huh, like O'Douls?"

"Ha, sort of yes."

"I wondered…" I stand up. "Well, thanks. And I hope I have the guts to take you up on your offer to…well…just talk, when the time comes."

"I'm not so scary am I?"

"No, no you're not, Father. I…appreciate that."

"Bill is fine…Just call me Bill."

"Oh, that's a tough sell, Father Bill. I don't know I could ever do that."

"Father's fine then, until you're ready. Let's go find those wayward kids huh?"

So we track down the kids, load'em in my old crew cab truck, all but Kelly. Kelly takes kind of a long time saying good night to Henry. I don't really want to push things, but Father says kinda loud, "You know, Dale, I have to get back pretty soon. I've got some calls to make yet tonight." He's a sharp old cuss, Father. Kelly comes back right away. We head on out, with Donny trying to get some teasing in and Kelly giving him some bad looks as we start to roll out the lake road. When we get back to Hunter, I drop Father at the base of College Hill about half a mile from St. Ann's and the…rectory; he says to let him out so he can walk up the hill under the moon. I don't ask no questions, figure it's somethin' religious. And then I head over to the house to get the kids to bed. I put a chew in and head down to the screen porch out front along the road. Like to just sit there some nights, even if I ain't livin' there for now. Well, I'll be gutted if Carrie ain't sittin' there on the swing seat waitin' for me.

"Hello, Dale."

"Well…Hello." I open the front door and spit the chew down into the shrub by the front steps, wiping' my face. "Get off early?"

"No, it's about right. I was just gonna sleep a little before you turned the rugrats back over to me."

"Well, why don't ya get some sleep?"

"Don't like my company?"

"No, no…I mean, yes, 'course I do. Just thought…"

"Father says you had a good day today…he just called me. Said maybe you and I should have a good talk."

"He's a nice fella."

"Yes, he is, Dale. I can't believe you didn't know that before."

"Well, I think I did. I just got caught up…in… Well, anyway Father and me got a deal now."

"So I hear."

"I gotta be honest, hon, I don't know it will work, but I think it's worth a try."

"I don't know if it will work either, Dale, but I think it's worth a try, too."

"So…what do you…think about me maybe stayin' a while?"

"I think we should try to make your good day into another one and take'em one at a time. If you want to stay over tonight with me…I think that would be…fine."

"And then?"

"And then, we'll see."

I sat down next to her. "That sounds nice, Carrie."

"Let's just sit for a minute more, here, listen to the night."

"Sounds good…"

"Dale, I've got somethin' else to tell ya. Funny how this all worked out."

"Uh oh…what's up?"

"I heard from Ike earlier today. First time in a while. He calls sometimes."

"Where is he?"

"I don't really know. I guess he'll tell us when he gets here."

"He's…he's comin' home?"

"Yeah. I don't know for how long. Don't know if it's just a visit."

"Well…that's, that's really good, ain't it?"

"Yes. He's got something on his mind though, you know how you could always tell, that kind of catch in his voice."

"You were always way better at understandin' him than I

was. Even when I wasn't off with the Puppies…"

She nods. "Yeah, well, trust me, he's got something to tell us, and there's something else too."

"What's that?"

"Well, he says he's not going to be alone."

"Well, sure, I guess Marie Jesson will be with him, and maybe…maybe…maybe a child?"

Carrie shook her head. Sounded like maybe she was holding back some tears, "No. He says Marie lost the baby, years ago…I just found this out today, still kind of shook up about it." She gives me a quiet look that makes me want to just take her in my arms. "…and then, after the baby was gone, he lost her. Hasn't seen her in over four years he said. They parted friends, I guess."

"Oh… oh….Carrie, I…didn't know." I kinda look away for a minute then back at her. "Doc Jesson know that?"

"He told me a thing or two about her last time I was in the vet's with Lester. Says she's doing okay. Somewhere out west. I think Montana. Met up with somebody and they're together. With what Ike told me the last couple times and especially today, I put two and two together."

"Well, that's too bad, about the baby mostly, I mean. The rest, well, that's up to them."

"About the baby, yes. Yes, it is. I wish he would have talked to me about it sooner. But, about Marie and him, well, I never really saw Marie and Ike staying together anyway."

"How come?"

"Just a feeling."

"Well, wait though…who's comin' with him?"

She shrugged. "I don't know. I guess we'll find out."

"When's he comin'?"

"He says Wednesday night." She grins at me. "So we can practice living in the same house until then."

I smile back. "That sounds really good, Carrie."

She leans over and kisses me. "I've missed you, Dale. Don't screw this up."

"I'll do my best…"

"No," she shakes her head, pulls me close, kind of hard, grabbin' my dirty old shirt in her strong, little hands. "I love you, Dale Sylvanus. Don't you screw this up!"

I swallow kind of hard. "Okay. It's a deal." I kiss her, then I stand up and open the inner porch door for her. She walks, through the doorway, into the house, across the front hall and starts up the stairs. She looks over her shoulder and smiles kinda gentle at me. I close the door behind me, real careful and quiet. Then, I follow her.

Monday, 6:01 a.m.

I smell coffee. I don't want to open my eyes because right now I have it in my head that I'm back home, and that Carrie took me back. If it's a dream, I don't wanna wake up. I don't wanna wake up and find I'm in some dive or in the boathouse, and Hughie is making some of his god awful coffee on a cookstove or some outdoor grill. Seems like dreams happen both ways. You have a awful one, and you wake up and you're glad, or like this one I might be havin': you have a great one and you wake up and it ain't true. That just kinda breaks your heart, and not in a little way, ya know?

But I open my eyes and I'm in my own bed. It's got kind of fancy blankets now that I been gone for a while, but I don't blame Carrie for that. That's the least she coulda done. I mean, she didn't never change the locks. She coulda did that. Course she'd have to put a actual lock on the back door first. Nobody steals nothin' in Hunter so far. Not even the college kids when they're here. Maybe that's 'cause if ya stold somethin' in Hunter, everybody would know who done it inside a hour. Now I can hear Carrie singin' down in the kitchen. She sings good. She was in the choir, when they had one for a year or two there, out at St. Brigid's on the lake, but then a couple members died and couple others sold off their lake places and well…it didn't take but three or four gone to leave nobody but Carrie singin' to Father Bill. Father's workin' lately on gettin' one goin' for the summers again. The college gots its own. St. Paul's choir. They sing for all different services. They got a chapel for about five different churches around on the campus. Most of the kids don't go to'em. Anyway, them kids in the college choir always sound good.

What's she singin'?

I think it's "Chuck E's in Love". Always liked that song, especially when Carrie sings it. She's been singin' it since we were kids. I remember she laughed at me one time when she heard me singin' it. I didn't really know it, 'cause it was big when me and Carrie were just little and I thought the words were "Chuck's easy love." She about wet herself when she heard me say that. I didn't get mad. Wasn't much point. She wasn't gonna stop laughin', and it was funny. Then she told me it'd been her Ma's favorite song too. She said her ma loved that song when she was pregnant with her. Her Ma died when Carrie was 10, hit by a drunk driver, sitting there by her mom's death bed was what got her goin' as a nurse. She was just broke all to pieces, Carrie says, and she remembers thinking that there ought to be some way she could help, at least ease the pain.

Anyway, she told me the singer of that song was Ricki Lee Jones. I told her I bet Big Ol' had his album 'cause he had all the oldies.

She laughed and said, "Ricki Lee Jones is a girl ya dope!"

Then she kinda brushed my hair back and kissed me. We were sittin' in Pop's truck at the time, down by the river. It was a summer night just like last night. I didn't mind her callin' me a dope. I didn't mind her callin' me anything, just so she stayed with me.

To this day, I've never got over the fact that Carrie wanted me. Here was this pretty girl off the Rez, all dark hair, dark eyes, and quiet smile, and she wanted me!

I remember so well when she first come to town. Everybody was wonderin' why this Indian girl had a Finnish name. Well, that came from her old man, of course, who was only a little bit Indian and didn't look it at all, but he'd lived on the rez with Carrie and her ma. He died too when Carrie was 20. I was just back from the service. I remember the funeral. Some folks from the tribe were there. The tribe is kinda Carrie's family, and they still act like that, but there ain't no direct relatives left. Kinda lonely for her, I think. That's what makes the way I been even worse. Anyway, Carrie and her dad come into town when Carrie's dad got a job at the college. Janitor. He'd been in the Indian fishing game before that. He had some Indian blood, like I said, so he was eligible to fish, especially 'cause his wife was full blood, but the college job paid more than fishing and was more regular. With just him to support Carrie, guess that was important.

Anyway, she was born before her Ma and Dad got married, just one a them things. Just like Ike for us. Like Carrie always says,

"Guess it was meant to be."

So, after her mom died and her pop got the job at Hunter Woods College, Carrie'd moved with him into Hunter and she'd took up with me. I sure wanted to keep her with me. She had lotsa options, big football players and all and she picked grubby ol' me. Well, one thing led to another and we got Ike. And now, after all I done to mess it up, she's picked me all over again. Well, I am sure as hell gonna try not to push my luck any more.

Anyway, this is a good mornin'.

Carrie is still singing Chuck E's in Love and I smile, rememberin' one time, about a year or so after that first kiss, when I went lookin' special for that song for Carrie's birthday, and I found the album in a record store in the Soo. Carrie liked that.

The door flies open and Lester comes in and jumps up on the bed and I cuss him out and I can hear Carrie laughin' down in the kitchen. Love that laugh. Gotta keep that laugh close. I'm aimin' to do just that. Hughie and the rest be damned.

I get myself outta bed and Lester licks my face, then Donny peeks around the corner.

"C'mon, Pop! Ma's makin' pancakes!"

Well, the pancakes are great. I think they woulda been even if Carrie had burnt'em, which she never does, just 'cause of where I am and how everything has changed so sudden like. Carrie's walkin' around in the kitchen which is just on the other side of the table. I built the table into the back side of the kitchen cabinet, that's around on her side. There's another cabinet that hangs down from the ceiling there, so there's a little slot in between them where you can hand plates out to the table or slide 'em across the marble top I put on the lower cabinet. Just like in a restaurant. I'm kinda proud of that. Hughie helped me with that design, and with buildin' it too. He's got a eye for the way things should go together. He's a good worker too, when he ain't stoned or drunk. I've had him out on a few jobs. Can't depend on him much, but I should talk I guess. She's walkin' around the kitchen still singin' Chuck E's in Love and Donny starts hummin' it too and I start laughin' thinkin' all the time "Chuck's easy love" and allofthesudden Carrie is leanin' down over the kitchen counter and lookin' at me with those dark eyes through the servin' slot and I know, you know? I know she knows exactly what I'm thinkin' and we just kinda share that and I almost start bawlin', and that woulda been hard to explain to Donny. Then she goes back to work, and walks around behind me and Donny at the table and calls up the stairs.

"Kelly, c'mon, I've got to get you over to art class, you're gonna miss it."

And a couple minutes later Kelly comes trudgin' down the stairs half asleep and I keep myself from laughin' but Donny starts right in on her.

"Oh look, Pop, it's awake! The creature is awake!" And he makes all kinds of funny noises and stomps around her as he sits down. And Kelly pulls her hair back, looks at me and kinda smiles. She's got a great smile. It's all her own. I don't recognize it from anybody else in the family. She smiles that smile and ya feel like she's a kid star or somethin', that you oughta ask her for an autograph. She's just glad I'm home, maybe and I think, how, how can I ever give this up just 'cause some awful things I saw give me a quiverin' in the belly? How can I give this up just for a few drinks and some laughs? I ain't never doin' it again. I decide that right then.

So, Kelly heads off to her class with one a them art professors from the college, private lessons I guess, in watercolors. I've seen some a what she does. She can make it real in some a them, but then she goes off paintin' some a them things that are just colors. I guess they're good too, but I wouldn't know. Over my head I think. I've seen Carrie just look at 'em when she don't know I'm watching and she just nods and sighs. See Carrie was good at art too, but she give it up a long time ago when she got pregnant with Ike. I think maybe for her birthday in October, I'm gonna give her a new paint set. Maybe clean out the attic make a studio up there where she and Kelly can both paint. I can do a lot of things for them, and I should, instead of hootin' and hollerin' out at the River House or wherever.

Well, got a busy day. Gotta get out to Chesterfield's and patch a hole in their roof, and clean them fish after that, and get 'em in the fridge. Then I gotta come back to the Hicks place in Hunter and crawl under the house. They got a skunk down there. Can't just shoot him or them if it's a family, 'cause it'll stink up the place. Gotta shew 'em away, close up the holes. That means I get to hear all the news from Jen Hicks. She's always got the stories. Used to work for the newspaper, so she goes on and on. Her brother, Doc O'Brian says she was always that way. Her husband Mark is a good fella. Psychologist. Talked to him a time or two after I got back from Afghanistan. Once on the VA's bill. Wasn't for me, but I could see he's good at it. Probably shoulda stuck with it, but now I got Father. Small towns are like that, everybody lookin' out for everybody even when yer bein' a damned fool. Maybe exspecially then. Course everybody's in your business too, but like Pop says, "Don't do nothin' you're ashamed of, then ya won't have any business to be in." Pop knows a lot. Saves it up and lets it out when somebody really needs it.

Up on the roof at Chesterfield's the mornin' is still foggy over the lake. This shouldn't take me too long. Shouldered a mess a shingles from the garage up here and a few sticks a wood for patches. Looks like it's just a leak along a seam, so a little caulk and some new shingles should do it. I patch that up in no time and I'm just comin' down the ladder when I see Henry Chesterfield comin' up to me eager.

"Hello, Mr. Sylvanus."

Polite kid. "'Dale's' just fine, Henry. Mr. Sylvanus is my Pop."

Henry nods. "Is…um…Kelly around today?"

"Well, believe she's around in Hunter, yeah." I look at my old Marine watch that I got in California when I was out there. "She's at a art class at the college. Should be done about now."

"Oh…good…" Henry kinda stammers around for a second. He's already got the news he wanted. I can't resist makin' him squirm a little.

"So you been seein' a lotta Kelly, have ya?"

"Well…well…just the last week or so…nothing…I mean…"

I keep myself from laughin'. "Well, you treat her good now, Henry. That's my little girl."

"Yes…yes sir."

"I know you will."

"Yes, sir." Henry gets outta there and on to his bike to ride down to Hunter, I suppose…fast as he can.

Soon as he's gone I wonder if I shoulda did that. Give the boy a hard time like that. Kelly might get sore at me. But I need to do that. Can't stop bein' careful, lookin' out for things. I learned that with Ike. And Kelly's a girl. My little girl.

I go inside and give the update to Old Man Chesterfield who is nice enough but kinda treats me like his little pet, talkin' to me like I don't know nothin'. Bugs me a little, but he don't mean no harm. When I go inside he's sittin' on the screened porch lookin' out at the lake holdin' a book about the history of the place in his hands. He's got them little half glasses on and a pair of new shorts and a bright yellow golf shirt. He's mostly bald. His wife is around upstairs lookin' at her antiques I bet. Nice folks really. I shouldn't be so picky.

"Hello Dale," the old man says. "All set up there?"

I smile the work man smile, "Well, we'll know with the next good rain, I guess, but I think so."

"Well that's good enough for me." He reaches into his pocket and pulls out a hundred and tries to hand it over. That's not usual. Usually, like Pop says you gotta wait for Christmas, get the check in the mail. Makes me wonder if maybe his wife has been after him about bein' cheap. She always pays me too much.

"Well, that's too much Mr. Chesterfield, it was just a little job…"

"Now Dale, you take that. You've got a family to feed." He holds up his book. "You ever read this?"

"No sir, can't say I have. I don't do a helluva a lot of readin', oh pardon the expression." That cuss was just to fit the mold. Gotta give 'em what they need as Pop says.

Mr. Chesterfield laughs, "No worries, Dale. No, the reason I mention it is lots of your people are mentioned in here."

"My people?"

"Yes, the Sylvanus family comes up over and over."

"Oh well yeah. I guess so. Pop could talk to ya about that. He knows all about the history."

"Does he? Janet and I will have to have them out some time. Mention it to your Dad will you?"

I try to imagine what that night would be like. "Sure, sure, Mr. Chesterfield."

I turn to go and he says, "Dale."

"Yes sir."

"I see our grandson Henry has been seeing your little... Kelly...is it?"

I smile. "I guess they have been, yes sir."

"Well, that's good. That's good. But you'll keep a watch on that for us, won't you."

"Sir?"

"You know, how these summer things are. Cute enough, puppy love and all..."

I start to turn red a little, but I guess his heart's in the right place, "Oh sure. She's my only daughter, but Henry seems like he's got his head on straight."

"Oh yes. Oh yes. His parents raised him right."

"Oh well, I can see that. We done our best with Kelly."

"Oh yes, oh yes. I know you have. I know that."

"Okay...well, give me a call if that roof leaks or any other thing."

He reaches out and shakes my hand. I force a smile and go out.

Don't know how to take what he said, maybe gettin' a thin skin, but I don't like nothin' bad said about my Kelly. She's a good girl. He probably didn't mean nothin'. Just watchin' out for his grandson until his folks get here. Still, kinda came off wrong in my mind.

To be fair I was just givin' Henry the third degree and kinda just for fun. So I don't know what I'm talkin' about...Ya gotta be a good dad, though. That's what I keep tellin' myself. Somethin' went wrong when I was raisin' Ike. And that worries me all the time I'm cleanin' and wrappin' the fish. Then I start wonderin' what he's got up his sleeve comin' back here after six years. Then I feel bad 'cause maybe he's just missin' home. And he's bringin' somebody with him. New girl maybe. Or…another kid? Could be anything really. We just don't know. I think Carrie's in the dark too. Seemed like she was wonderin' what was goin' on just like me. Well, the next house I'm goin' to is the place to find out the scoop. If there's somethin' to know about somebody in Hunter, Jen Hicks knows it.

When I get there Mark is headin' off to start his shift at the prison in Newberry. He's the chief head shrinker there, I guess. He's in their little half circle brick driveway, that I put in for him last summer, just about to get into his red Jeep.

"Hey, Dale. Gonna take care of our stinky pal?"

"Well, I hope so. Maybe without stinkin' up your house."

"Just make sure he doesn't get you."

We both have a laugh. "Well, have a good one. Jen's just finishing up her coffee. She's bursting to tell you some things, like usual."

I smile. "Oh now…"

"Ha, we both know it's true, God love her."

"Have a good one."

"You too."

He pulls away and the door flies open and Jen is in the yard already talkin' to me, "What's this I hear about you and Carrie?"

I laugh. She does get the scoop quick. "Well…"

"Back together are you?" She is kinda leanin' forward waitin' for me to say somethin'. She's all dressed up nice already this morning. Her hair is pulled back in a tight kinda bun. She's skinny as a rail. Always movin'. Doc O'Brian says he gets tired just watchin' her. I get what he means.

"Well, I kinda hope so, Mrs…." she kinda eyes me up, we've been through the name thing before. She gets downright mad at me if I don't call her by her first name, "…Jen. We only got around to gettin' back together just around midnight last night. I guess we'll stay together if I don't…screw it up." I didn't really want to talk about it, thought I might jinx it, but Jen Hicks has a way of bringin' it outta ya. She don't mean no harm, and she near always does good things with what she finds out. No question she's nosy though.

"Well, that's sweet. Just sweet! Did I hear right, that your Ike is coming home this week too?"

Now how in the world does she know that? As far as I know the only way Carrie knows that is from the phone call she got. I don't say anything so she kinda like reads my mind I think, "I heard that from Ike's friend Jason Willis, in the grocery store." She sighs a little bit, "He was in there buying some of that stupid apple beer and a bunch of chips. I bawled him out for not taking care of himself. I don't know what's going to become of him. His mother just shakes her head if you bring him up."

I'm only half listening. Finally I say, when she watches me for a coupla seconds, "Well, ya, Ike's supposed to be here Wednesday."

Jen kinda leans towards me holdin' her coffee, puts a hand on my shoulder, "Mark and I were so sorry to hear about the baby, but I guess in the long run it worked out, though it must have been awful hard for both of them."

Now I really don't know what to say, so I just stay quiet.

"Oh my gosh. My big mouth. You didn't know?"

"Well…we just found out yesterday. Happened a long time ago."

"Yes, yes, but…but… that's always hard. Oh, I'm sorry. My big… But now Marie's got a new life with her…wife…out there in Montana. So, good things come, don't they?" She looks at me and I'm sure I got no expression 'cause it's all just washin' over me. Finally she says, "Guess the other girl, Janey is her name, comes from a big ranch family?"

"Um…what?"

Jen turns kinda red. "Well, I guess I really put my foot in it…"

"No, no, go ahead…"

"Well…yes, Marie figured out she was a lesbian after she and Ike broke up. Called him and apologized for givin' him…

such a… Moved off to Montana and met this Janey, what…four years ago?" She stares at me again and I'm just frozen. "Colleen… Jessen… told me that."

I just kind of stand there, staring out at the morning for a minute.

"Oh, oh, I guess I've done a number on you. So sorry, Dale."

I stand there tryin' to get my head around it. Finally somethin' comes out… "No, no, it's okay. So…I better get after this skunk."

"Sure, sure. You know where the crawlspace is, huh?"

"Ya, sure. I put it in for ya." I manage a smile. "I guess I should."

Then somethin' hits me, and I figure, even though not even a third of it all has sunk in yet, as long as I'm filled in on everything else, I might as well out and ask her this too.

"Say, Mrs.…Jen, Ike says he's bringin' somebody with him when he comes, you know anything about that?"

"Why…no….that's interesting. I bet I could find out if you want." She perks up.

Oh boy, what did I just do? "Oh…no…no…" but I can see it's already too late. She's just itchin' to get back on her computer, or phone or whatever and find out about that. I'm a dope. "Never, mind. I guess I'd just as soon find out on Wednesday when Ike gets here."

"No trouble…"

"No, no, really. Thanks. I better get to work."

"Okay."

Jen Hicks is a funny lady. She's a very good person, but she just can't help findin' out everything. Probably never shoulda quit her newspaper job. Well, this time she's sure given me a bunch to think about. That must be what Carrie meant about not seein' Ike and Marie together. I think maybe she know'd about that. Why can't I never see none of this stuff, when it's right in front of me? Just thick I guess. Truth is I used to make jokes about faggots and lesbos all the time myself. Especially when I was first in the

Marines. Everybody done it. Never thought about'em bein' people, especially not anybody I knowed. Just seemed like characters in a joke. Not real. I made a joke like that one time in front of Carrie and she sat me down and explained some things to me about how some folks are just like that. She was talkin' to me like a nurse, ya know? Just matter of fact. It's like a skin color or eye color or bein' left handed or whatever, she says. It's just the way folks are she says. I thought it over and it kinda made sense. We always knew who was like that in our classes, I guess, though I don't think none of us really believed it. It was just a way of bein' mean. Kids are so mean, ya know. Especially when they're growin' up. And what must it be like for them folks? All of us makin' mean fun, just to kill time? Kinda makes me feel bad about all the mean stuff I said to'em. I try to make it seem not so bad 'cause I was just a kid, even in the service, but when I think about it, I know'd it wasn't nice even then. 'Course I'd never bring none a that up, about Ike and Marie, or about folks havin' feelin's like that and all around the Puppies; they ain't ever gonna get their heads around this.

And now it's right in our own family sort of. But I guess that ain't new neither. Uncle Joshua was like that. He died of the AIDs in California back in the 80s. Ma and Pop went out for the funeral. He was Ma's brother. It was real sad she said. Come to think of it, I don't know I ever thought about him bein'…what…gay… until just now.

I don't know. I don't know. Hard to keep up.

And who is Ike bringin' home? Makes me want to go back into the house here and hurry Jen up to find out. I guess, though, if Ike wants it secret until he gets here, we better keep it that way.

So, I crawl in under the house. Turns out there ain't no skunk residin' in there so to say, but he is going in and out. So I patch up best I can all around, fix up some a the insulation and caulk some spots. When I come out Jen is standin' there waitin' for me. I can tell she knows somethin', but she ain't gonna tell unless I ask. So I don't ask. I just tell her all's well under there now and to call if the skunk shows up again. She pays me and I can tell she's just itchin' to be asked. But I just wave bye and head out after she pays me. I can feel her still watchin' me, just waitin' for a opportunity when I leave.

I swing over to our house and Carrie is there. Opens the front door as I walk up.

"Just in time for lunch!"

"Great!"

We head in for the kitchen, and my phone rings. I see it's Hughie so just let it ring.

"Who's that?"

"Hughie."

"Aren't you going to answer it?"

"He's just tryin' to get me to go drinkin'. Probably knows I got some money in my pocket from the jobs this morning."

That reminds me and I pull the bills out of my pocket and give 'em to Carrie. Then I walk over to the fridge and put the fish in the freezer.

"Don't you need some of this?"

"Next couple days I don't want any of it. Easier to deal with Hughie if I can say honest that I ain't got none."

"Oh…you think he'll be after you that much?"

"Trust me. Less temptation for me too if I don't have it."

"You know what's best." She smiles at me.

"I know all right, but I ain't always done it."

"That's over, Dale. Every day can be like today if you want it to be."

"I know it." I kinda take a breath and I don't know if I'm happy or sad or scared or mad or what I am. Carrie kinda rubs my back, kisses me on the cheek, looks me over.

She sets a BLT on the kitchen table, and I'm still full from this morning but I wolf it down pretty fast.

"Carrie, you got any idea who Ike's bringin' with him?"

She shakes her head. "No. I have guesses."

"What would ya guess?"

"New girlfriend, maybe even a wife."

"That's what I'm thinkin'. So how come he doesn't just tell us that?"

"Lot of reasons, I guess. He's hard to know, especially when we haven't seen him in so long."

"Six years."

"Long time. Wonder how he looks."

"Probably filled out."

Carrie turns away for a second. It's hard for a Ma not to see her kids. Harder than for a Dad, I think. Don't know why.

"Did you know that stuff about Marie being a lesbian?"

"Well…yes. I've known for quite a while to be honest. How did you… Oh, you were over at Hicks' house."

"Got the scoop. I think maybe she knows who Ike's bringin' with him too. You wanna ask her or should I ask her?"

"Jen is a pistol…No, I guess if Ike wants to tell us himself, or show us, we should let him."

"That's what I thought too."

"You think pretty well. Even if you don't think so."

She smiles at me again, and that alone makes my day. The kids ate before I did and they're doin' what kids do in the summer and we both feel the mood, so we go up to the bedroom for a while. Ain't done that for some time, especially not in the day. Nice.

After that I fix some little things around the house, some that don't even need fixin' just so I can be around Carrie. It's funny, other guys I know, including all of the pups even Big Ol' talk about how they'd like to trade the wife in on a younger model, well… except for Big Ol' all the pups already did, them that had a model to begin with anyway…in Hughie's case…it was funny. He didn't never seem to have no luck with women. Just fought with'em or was like their buddy or somethin'. There was that Marjorie, and they were gettin' serious I thought, but one day he said he wasn't seein' her no more. Said she said somethin' pissed him off and that was that. No woman was gonna run his life.

Anyway, Carrie just seems better to me all the time. She's smart. She's funny. She's pretty. And she don't take my crap, or anybody's crap. Best of all, in spite of all the dumb stupid stuff I done, she really loves me. Guess this just boils down to I love my wife and I'm damned glad to be back with her. Don't know what I was thinkin'.

About two Carrie's phone rings and her face just lights up after she says hello. It's Ike I can tell. I'm there putterin' away with some dials on the stove, tryin' to get'em tight again.

"Sure," Carrie says and her smile has gotten real big and her dark eyes are just flashin' as she walks the phone over to me, her head just noddin' at what I ain't sure. She hands me the phone.

"Hello?"

"Hi, Dad."

"Ike…"

"Yeah, it's me, Dad."

"Well…well son I'm just so…glad to hear you."

"It's…it's good to hear you too…"

"So…I guess we'll see you soon, huh?"

"Yeah…yeah…we'll be coming in Wednesday. I kinda wanted to tell you something."

"Oh…oh…good…I mean, shoot, go ahead…"

"Well, I'm married. Just got married."

"Oh…well…congratulations! Anyone…we know?" Maybe shouldn't have said that. Not sure why.

"No, nobody you know. But I know you'll like her, Dad. And well…it's kind of important to me that you do."

"Well…sure…that's good… Sure I will. Thanks, Ike. I'm… just…just real happy for you, son."

There's a little laugh on the other end of the line. "Oh… okay. Well, that's great, Dad. I'm…looking forward to being there…I…well, I understand some things now, I think. Some of the things that happened when I was little. Maybe…maybe I even get you a little better. And I just…I just wanted to say…even before I got there…that I'm sorry. I'm sorry I didn't get it. I was just a kid…"

"Now Ike that's all past. I ain't…I'm just glad to… hear you…"

"Yeah…well…I know you've probably been hearing all kinds of rumors. It hasn't all been good. I haven't always been good is what I'm saying. But, but that's all behind me now. I've got a wife, and Dad, she's got a little girl…well, we do, really. The girl is ours. She's mine too…um…biologically."

"Oh…oh…Ike well that's sweet…"

"Just…just let me finish and then you can put Ma back on the line…"

"Okay. Sure."

"Well…she isn't going to be quite what you're used to. Just be ready that she's going to be different, both she and her girl…" In the background I hear a woman's voice say, 'Our girl'. "Our girl, like I said she's mine too… And I just…"

I knew then he was trying to tell me not to say anything dumb around them. It hurt a little, but I swallowed it down. "Ike… it's okay. I get ya. I…I can't wait to meet'em…And, son, you're gonna see I ain't the same as I was when you left…" I didn't know where that came from. Maybe just from these last two days. From talkin' to Carrie and Father Bill. Maybe I've just got too old for kiddin' myself, too old not to tell people the truth. "I…I ain't so quick to think I know everything no more…I'm just, so happy yer comin'…" I wanted to say more, that I been worried about'em, that I love'em…that I didn't give a crap who he married long as it made him happy…but that part stuck in my throat and all that came out was…"…well…that's it really…I'm really tryin'…you'll see."

"Well…okay…that sounds…nice. I, well, I've really missed you, Dad. There were a lot of times I wanted to call you…but I was just…afraid…No, that didn't come out right."

"No…no…I get it, Ike. Really. We're…we're good. Just come home and we can talk some more if you want…"

"Well Dad, that sounds really good…"

"Here's, here's your Ma…" I hand her the phone and walk into the livin' room and I think I'm gonna throw up for a second and I got no idea why and I turn on the TV and sit there gawkin' at some soap opera not really seein' what's on the screen. Hopin' I didn't say nothin' stupid, but pretty sure I did. I'm sittin' there for a while and then Carrie comes in without me hardly noticin' and she wraps her arms around my neck and kisses me on the ear.

"Did…did…I screw up?"

"No! No, Dale you did just right. Why did you think…?"

I turn and look at her and she says, "You're cryin'…:

"Well, well…" I say, and wipe away a tear I didn't even know was there. And I wonder what the hell's happenin' to me. "I guess there's a first time for everything."

An hour or so goes by and I ignore a couple more calls from Hughie. Then he calls again, and I'm out in the yard rakin' up some a Lester's work and some dead leaves and sticks on the back of the lot. Carrie's left for her shift. She won't be back until midnight. The phone rings again, and sure enough it's Hughie and I figure why not just talk to him 'cause he ain't gonna stop.

"Hello, Hughie."

"Now just hear me out."

I smile despite it all…maybe 'cause he don't have a chance now. I got my wife back. My boy is comin' back. No fun with the Pups is even close to comin' up to that.

"Go ahead…"

"We got a keg. Left over from Shine's niece's wedding. We brought it out to Chessy's lot down by the river. You know the one…We can fish and just lazy back and have some beer right on the shore. No crazy stuff…"

"Sounds nice, Hughie."

"Oh, good! Yer, yer comin' then?"

The sound in his voice is like a little boy's. It's like listenin' to Donny… I used to say no to Donny and Ike and Kelly all the time. Now it's Hughie's turn.

"No, Hughie, I ain't comin'…"

"C'mon, just for one…"

"No, now really listen this time, Hughie. I ain't comin' this time. I ain't comin' any time from now on."

There's a lotta quiet for a long time, then, "Big talk…"

He's makin' it easier. I wonder if he knows that. "You can just stop callin' here if that's all ya want. I got my wife back. In a couple days I'm gonna have my boy back. Hughie, I just talked to'em on the phone…first time in six years. You, you don't know how important..."

"Well, well, okay. But he ain't coming for a couple days right?"

"Wednesday."

"Okay, so why can't ya have a couple beers with the Pups today?"

For just a moment, just a moment, I hesitate...

"No."

"Dale, you act like we got the plague or somethin'. I've known you since..."

"Kindergarten, that's right, Hughie. And you're gonna say ya got my back. And...well...I know you think that's true, but if I come there it will be fun and I won't stop at one or ten, or twenty and we'll be off on a nasty ripper before I know it..."

"Well that don't sound so...Lots of time until Wednesday..."

"No!"

"Oh...well ya don't have to yell. You on the rag or what?"

"No, I mean, Hughie there ain't lotsa time. That's what these last couple days...That's what I got in my head now. There just ain't lotsa time. What...what do ya really care about, Hughie...?"

"Huh?"

"What do ya really care about?"

"Okay, Padre...we'll just let this one..."

"No. Are you my friend, Hughie?"

"Can't believe you said..."

"Are ya...?"

"Ya. Ya, Dale. I'm your friend. Always was. And...and... what do I care about? I care about you. I care about the Pups."

I didn't see that one comin'. But somethin' comes into my head. "Well...maybe if ya care about the Pups, Hughie, the Pups gotta just stop bein' the Pups..."

"You don't mean that. I'll give ya a couple days..."

"It ain't gonna matter...Hughie...If ya care about somebody, ya gotta use your time ta...make sure they're okay..."

"Dale, you okay?"

"Yeah, Hughie. That's what I'm tellin' ya. My bein' okay

means I ain't runnin' with you guys no more. I'm not just sayin' that. I really mean it."

"Oh come off it Padre, you like it just as much as I do…"

"More."

"What?"

"More, Hughie. I like it way more than you do. That's why…if yer my friend…ya gotta leave me alone." Then somethin' else came into my head. "And…and if I ever say yes, or show up at the River House when I know yer there or just come and join ya…if yer really my friend…ya gotta tell me to get lost. Ta go back to Carrie. Ya gotta force me into a car and drive me home. Hughie, I'll know yer really my friend when that happens…"

The phone goes dead.

Where did that come from? That's what I'm thinkin'. And I'm wonderin' who was talkin' for me. Father Bill? Carrie? Pop? Ma? Somebody else, 'cause I ain't never heard that guy before. And I suddenly see I'm sweatin' and I'm breathen' hard, and all of a sudden all I want to do is get in my damned old truck and run out to that place by the river and throw back about ten beers and whatever else somebody hands me or I can afford, and that roadside in the desert comes rollin' back into my head and that kid with his legs blowed off screamin' and I try to think of Ike on the phone and Carrie and I start walkin' towards the truck and the phone rings.

It's Father Bill.

"Dale. I was just up in the steeple. You got the heavy stuff out, but the walls and the floor and the ceiling need to be scrubbed out if ya can. No hurry just…"

"No, no, I'll come now. I'll come right now."

"Well, like I said no…"

"No, right now will be good."

"Oh…"

"I'm in the truck, be there in ten minutes."

"Oh…then I'll stay here."

"I…I think that might be good."

"Come right away."

"I am. Okay."

I hang up and I put down the phone. I get into the truck and I start it up. You know how in them old movies there's like a angel on a guy's one shoulder and a devil on the other? Well, I swear to ya that's kind of the way it is. Only my devil is a kid, just a kid dressed up in a soldier's uniform, screamin' by a dusty roadside and Hughie laughin' and drinkin' down a shot. And on the other shoulder is Father Bill noddin' and holdin' the phone: waitin' and Carrie, Donny, Kelly, and Ike all huddled together lookin' at me. And I get out to the road and if I turn right it's that place by the river for sure until the keg is nothin' but foam, and who knows after that maybe disappearin' for five or six days and missin' Ike completely and maybe pissin' off Carrie permanent. So I turn left, but all the way up the hill and out on the highway and down to the lake turn off and almost right to the church there's a voice sayin' clear as that steeple bell, "You can turn back. You can turn back. All you're gonna get here is a lecture." And the sun is shinin' through the trees and what kind of a day is this to be sittin' in a church, shovelin' bat shit when I could be droppin' a line in the river and havin' a couple innocent cold ones, and I almost turn around, but then right in the parkin' lot there's Father Bill. Smilin' without showin' his teeth almost kinda smilin' with his body if that makes any sense, and he acts like a parkin' lot attendant at a ballgame and kinda waves me into a parking space on the gravel, right next to his little car. And I sit in the driver's seat for a minute and kinda take a breath. And I notice Father don't open the door for me. He just stands there lookin' kinda hopeful through the window almost like Donny. And I see what he's sayin' by standin' there, even though he ain't sayin' a word, "It's gotta be your idea, Dale." Is the message. And it is my idea. For once it is, and I get out.

"Have you got some extra scrub brushes, Dale?"

"Huh?"

"That bell tower looks like a two man job."

"Oh, sure, Father. I was thinkin' maybe I could get up with a mop too and maybe clean off the ceilin' and the bell, even."

"Good idea."

And so we go at it and collect everything we need from the

out buildings and we go up there with a whole bunch of buckets
of bleach and water and brushes and mops and paint scrapers, and
everything I could lay my hands on and we don't say a thing to
each other and we just work like slaves up there for four hours. And
finally when we're just standin' there, about to go down the ladder,
Father Bill says, "Good and clean."

"Huh?"

"Good and clean. Good hard work. I don't do enough of it.
I need to remember to get my hands dirty. Sweat. Sometimes that's
the best way to get out of your own way. I wish I could remember
that more. Everything I read tells me that, but it's funny, it sort of
contradicts itself just by being there on the page. It's like everything
I read in the Bible and in the great religious writings tells me to
close the book and get out there and do good work and rest only
when you're tired."

"I don't know if I understand all that, Father. Except that
part about bein' tired."

"You better get on home to Carrie. It's 6:30. She's going to
think you're…gone off. Here's a little something I wanted to give
you." He hands me a piece of paper folded up real careful. "Read
this if you ever can't get ahold of me when you need to."

I take it and stick it in my pocket. Then I stand there kinda
awkward. "Don't we need to talk, Father?"

"I think we already did. Just not with words. I'm listening
though, if there's something else."

I think about it for a second and I can feel a smile buildin'.
None of them devils are talkin' anymore. I just wanna get home for
supper.

"Little bit of hard work? That's all it takes, Father?"

"Well…this time."

"What about next time?"

"Well, you call me again and we'll try whatever works.
How about that?"

"Thank you Father….you're…a very good man."

"Nope. Don't start that. I'm a man, and my name is Bill.
Now get on home to Carrie. Need me to come with you, make

sure you make it?" He smiles, but I can see underneath that he ain't really kiddin'.

"No. I'll make it…Bill"

"That's the way. Call right away if you need me again, even if it's on the way home."

"I will."

We climb back down and Father offers to help me put everything away, but I wave him off and he starts up his car and heads back home and I'm there twenty or so minutes more. And, just before I leave, here come the Pups blastin' on in in Shine's old Chevy and I kinda breathe a breath and just as they get out the phone rings and it's Carrie.

"Dale, honey, come home."

"I'm comin' right now, hon…"

"I…I saw Shine's Chevy go by…"

"Yup, they're standin' right in front of me. I was cleanin' out the bell tower with Father."

She laughs a sad little laugh. "That's a good name for it."

And for a second I really don't get it, and then, I catch on to what she means. "Ha…that's a pretty good one. I'm good hon, really. I'm comin' home. Be right there." I hang up the phone and look Hughie right in the eyes.

Hughie starts in on me holdin' out a pint of "Wild Turkey" but I shake my head, try to get into the truck. He blocks me. He's really startin' to piss me off.

"One shot. What can it hurt?"

"Everything. This is really hard for me Hughie…but get the hell away from me."

Shine and Chessy are kinda shufflin' in the dirt behind Hughie and they both kinda look away when I look at them. They never been very brave souls. Truth all around.

"Oh, the Padre's swearin'. Better watch out Carrie and Father might spank ya!" Hughie says.

Chessy gives a little dumb laugh and I glare at him and he looks away.

"Hughie, I meant what I said before. I'm goin' home. Be a

friend, huh? Leave me be?" I walk around him and get in the truck. Hughie grabs the door.

"You ain't no better than us."

"No I ain't, Hughie, I'm worse, but I'm tryin' to be better." I kinda slowly pull the door shut and Hughie lets go of it. I think he's surprised more than anything. I am too.

I don't look back when I pull away, because even right now I feel like it would be good to go off with 'em. I wonder when that feeling is gonna go away. I wonder if it ever will. Something in Father Bill's eyes when he told me he was a drunk tells me it won't. So I just have to keep workin' at it every day. That sounds damned hard. Pop always says ya can't get somethin' for nothin'. And when I think about it, I stand to gain a lot. My wife back after six months. My son back after six years. And still, just drinkin' some beer or downin' some shots and headin' off who knows where to do who knows what seems better than Ike or Carrie, or even just feelin' good about myself. How can that be? I don't know. It's a long road I guess. And I start down it right then, startin' up the truck and never lookin' back, for fear I'll ditch it all again.

★★★

Back at home… It sounds good to say that. Back at home, for dinner we have the fish and some others that were in the freezer and it goes nice. The kids are in a good mood and not fightin' with each other for once and after dinner they're just out playin' with their friends in the yard, along our quiet street, while Carrie and me sit on the porch swing. I could just stay here like this forever.

"Well…" she says. "Back to work soon."

"You on midnight?"

She nods. She works hard, but I know she likes the work. Feels like she's doin' somethin' important. That's 'cause she is.

"You going to be okay tonight Dale?"

I don't say nothin' for a second. "Yeah…"

"Why the big pause?"

"Oh…I dunno…"

"This isn't going to be easy, Dale."

"I been thinkin' that. Makes me mad though."

"What does?"

"Well, it should be easy. If I can just stay away from the Pups I've got you and the kids, and now even Ike. That should be easy as hell and well…it just ain't…"

"Oh honey. I know it isn't. You're fighting something most people never get over."

"What…the war stuff?"

"Well, sure. And you're tryin' to break habits that maybe you need some help to break. Addiction…"

"Well, I'm not so sure it's…"

"Well, maybe not booze, but something. Why else would it be so hard? Are you getting some help?"

I nod. "Talked to Father Bill today."

"What did he say?"

"Not much really…oh…he gave me somethin'…"

"What?"

"I don't know."

She laughs. "You're a funny guy. What did he give you?"

I reach in my pocket. "This piece of paper."

Now she's laughin' and I start too. I take it out and read it.

"What's it say?"

I hand it to her 'cause I don't read so good out loud. She looks it over and kinda nods. Sighs a little bit. Then she reads it out loud: "My Lord God, I have no idea where I am going. I do not see the road ahead of me….Therefore will I trust you always though I may seem to be lost and in the shadow of death. I will not fear, for you are ever with me, and you will never leave me to face my perils alone. Let all the people say 'Amen'."

"Amen." I say. 'Cause I don't know what else to do.

Carrie smiles at me. "Father Bill is a pretty sharp character."

"That somethin' he made up on his own you think?" She hands me back the paper.

"No, it says 'Thomas Merton' at the bottom. He's a famous monk, I think."

"I didn't know monks got famous."

She laughs. She kisses me. Then she goes upstairs to shower

and get dressed.

I put the paper back in my pocket. I'm glad I have it. I don't know what the next couple days are gonna bring. I should be free from Hughie and the Pups at least for a while, unless one a them gets a wild hair and decides to pay a midnight visit. Never know. I wouldn't be that mad if they did, but it'd be hard to get them outta here without wakin' up the kids. Guess, if they show I'll meet'em in the yard. Maybe I should sleep on the porch to keep them from hollerin' for me. But if I go out there, how am I gonna stop myself from gettin' in the car with'em? I kinda finger the paper in my pocket. It's good just ta know it's there. And I can call Father. Bill. I'd hate to do that in the middle of the night, but he made it pretty clear I can call any time.

I open up the screen door. "It's 10:30. Time to come in."

Kelly and Donny say goodbye to their friends and kinda gradual work their way in. I remember what that was like from bein' a kid. You just had a good day and you don't want it to end. You almost think there won't ever be another one like it. You may be right. But there's a lotta days and most of 'em are good in some way or other. This day's had its ups and downs. But maybe the bad parts are gonna turn into good. And talkin' to Ike on the phone was good. Doin' the work with Father Bill was good. Bein' with Carrie and the kids was…well… great, so I guess this one ranks right up there. Ma used to tell me to count my blessin's before I went to bed. I guess I'm doin' that now. And this little piece of paper in my pocket with the famous monk's writin' on it, might help. Seems like good advice. Just have a little faith. And I guess maybe a little faith can lead to a lot of good things. I dunno. Ha! Maybe I am turnin' into a preacher.

So, I get the kids to bed. Donny kinda runs at me and hugs me before he goes off up stairs. Tells me he loves me. Well, that should keep me here a while, I hope. Kelly doesn't say that much, but I can see she's glad I'm here too. Carrie heads off about quarter after eleven. Kisses me. I see her kinda hesitate a second.

"Be good now."

"I'm tryin'."

"Don't try. Be good. Hughie shows up…tell him. Tell him to go fuck himself."

She turns away I think half cryin'. She don't wanna leave. I don't blame her.

I say to her, "I'll be right here."

"Promise?" she says.

"Promise." I says. "Love ya."

"Love you."

She turns back to me one more time then heads for her car walkin' around the house and out back.

I hear it start up and see it go down the road from the corner.

After that, I just don't seem able to sleep so I go and find my sleepin' bag and lay it out on the screen porch. Half waitin' for the Pups to show up, half watchin' the night. There's some coyotes around the edge of town. They walk right through big as life at night sometimes. They're after bunnies and deer what don't make the muster. They're doin' their job I guess.

It's funny to see the night sober. Straight as a judge. I try to settle in, in the sleepin' bag, but the time just keeps passin' slow like. One thing I don't wanna do is get up and start wanderin' around town, or worse, go on out to my truck. Gotta stay here. Gotta stand guard maybe… Maybe that's the way to think of it, but that makes me think of the service. And that brings me back to that roadway.

I reach into the pocket a my pants. They're on the floor. I pull out that paper, "My Lord God, I have no idea where I am going…" Ya. That's it. That's how I feel. And if this famous monk felt that way too, I guess I ain't alone. I guess there's a whole bunch of us awake in the night all the time. Tryin' to make some sense of it maybe. Just tryin' to be safe, keep those folks we love safe. Maybe we're a kinda army too. Like a army of the night all thinkin' we're alone when we're not.

This famous monk was maybe the head of the army. Maybe Father Bill's another one of the officers. Maybe Big Ol' is a sergeant. Me, I'm just a jarhead like always.

And who are the enemies? I could say folks like Hughie

and Chessy, and Shine are, but that ain't fair really. They're just grunts like me, tryin' to find their way too, but makin' the wrong choices just like I done for years and years.

It's about choices, I think. Every second yer alive, just makin' the right choices, then goin' on from there. But this thing Father Bill brung me kinda makes me feel better. I ain't alone. I ain't the only one makin' the hard choices. I dunno. Seems to make sense, but then a lotta stuff makes sense when yer half awake, that just seems dumb in the light a day. Maybe that's okay, though. Maybe there's a kinda night sense and a day sense and one don't have much ta do with the other. You gotta have both maybe. Like the way Pop says ya gotta treat the summer lake people, put on a little show for'em. Not quite like that, though. 'Cause this ain't no show. It's real. It's right where ya are.

I roll over and look out towards the street. I hear a bad muffler roarin' around the corner. Here come the Pups. The Chevy comes around the corner bobbin' and weavin'. I just stay put.

It comes up to a stop right out front. I almost get up to shut them up. Window in the back seat rolls down. I hear Hughie's voice whispering', "Ahh, he ain't up. He's turned pussy maybe fer good. Let's go."

I hear the driver's window come down, "Padre, you Pussy!" That's Shine. He don't say nothin' until he gets drunk, then you can't shut him up.

"Shut up, Shine ya fuckin' idiot. Let's go. He ain't comin'."

The Chevy rolls away. I roll over. Hope they don't come back. Truth? Truth is if they'd a got out and come up here I don't know what I woulda done. Maybe woulda talked myself inta goin' with'em just to keep'em safe. Talked myself into some shit like that. Glad they kept goin'. Funny they did really. I get the feelin' it weren't Hughie's idea to come here. Huh. That's somethin'. Maybe he's learnin'. Maybe he's part a the light night army too. Keepin' watch his own way. Watchin' out for me. Like to think that's true. We been friends a long time.

After midnight I drift off again. Some time in the night I wake up screamin'. Musta had the dream about the kid in

Afghanistan again, but I don't remember. I listen in the house and don't hear the kids. I don't hear the Chevy around either, so they musta headed for Newberry or the Soo. Either way, I just hope they make it back.

I think about Carrie off workin' with her patients. All them folks are dyin'. I wonder how they sleep or if they do. I know Carrie does what she can to comfort them. Hell of a job. I couldn't do it. She's tough. Lots tougher than me. She sees things clear all the time. I'm the only thing that confuses her, I think. Me and Ike. Hate to think he's the way he is 'cause a me, but I know, no matter how many different ways I look at it, that it's my fault he's that way and I'll have to live with it forever. Hope he forgives me.

He sounded good on the phone, though. It'll be good ta see him. Meet this new wife. Wonder about that. And his daughter. My granddaughter! He seemed pretty worried. Why wouldn't I like her? The wife? Who am I ta say somebody ain't up to snuff anyway? I ain't no prize.

I get up and open the inner porch door careful. I close it behind me and walk out through the front hall, through the living room, and into the kitchen. Grab some orange juice out of fridge. I drink it, standin' right there on the linoleum in my bare feet. It makes me think of drinkin' a screwdriver. Dumb. Seems like it oughta be the other way around. I dunno.

Lester follows me back out to the porch. Stinky ol' dog. Nice though. Gives me some company. Lies down by me when I get back in the sleepin' bag. Helps me watch the rest of the night.

Last thing I remember before I finally drift off is him snorin'.

Tuesday, 9:33 a.m.

Whoa! Slept a long time once I finally got down. Carrie wakes me up when she gets off shift. She's been lookin' around the house for me for a while. Thought the worst. Don't blame her.

"Whatcha doin' out here?" she says.

"If the Pups showed up I wanted to shut them down before they woke the kids."

She looks at me kinda uneasy. She's testin' the story, I think. Lot of reason to, needless to say. "Did they…show up?"

"Yup, but they left when they didn't see no lights. I didn't have to do nothin'."

"Huh…funny. They usually don't give up." She's lookin' in my eyes real hard.

"Yeah…I thought so too." I say.

She nods, but now I figure Carrie's thinkin' the truth over just like me. What are the Pups up to? After a minute or two, straightenin' things up, pickin' up my dirty socks, what not, she says, "Want some breakfast?"

"Well…sure…but don't you need to sleep?"

"Can't yet, still charged up."

"I know how that is. Not like a nurse, but I know about…" No point goin' there. "…sure I'll have breakfast."

We go on out to the kitchen and put together some eggs and toast. No sign of the kids and there won't be for a while so we just sit down and eat our breakfast at the kitchen table. Carrie kinda sighs. I look up.

"This is nice," she says. "Just an ordinary day. Us waiting for the kids to get up."

"You don't have to wait, I can clean this up."

"No, I've got the day off. Tomorrow too, for Ike. I'll sit up a while and then catch up after the kids go off to do whatever."

I take a look out the window but don't see nothin' but gray skies, my truck out by the garage, and some loose shingles on the roof out there. Another project. That's good.

"Supposed to rain today. I was gonna paint over at Brown's,

but I may not be able to."

"Well, make sure you call and tell them you're not coming."

That grates a little. Of course I'm gonna call, but when I was still runnin' with the Pups, I mighta forgot. Might not a called 'em for days. Then been afraid to call 'em. Then too lazy. Then too drunk. Keep goin' like that for weeks sometimes 'till I lost the job. Most folks around here are so nice they'd let me go a while. Someplace else? I wouldn't never have no work actin' like that.

"Yup…I'll call."

"I wonder what he looks like now."

She lost me a bit there, but we been married so long we can usually pick up what the other one is thinkin' after a bit.

"Ike…ya mean?"

"Who else?"

"I dunno. Hope he looks like you."

"I hope he's handsome like his father." She kisses me and picks up the dishes.

My phone rings and at the same time Pop comes in the front door.

"Well…I don't smell no puppy poop!" Pop says. He's talkin' about Hughie and the Pups a course. He don't like them much, but always puts it in a friendly way. Truth? He'd help them guys out of a jam same as me, but he don't like my runnin' with 'em. Come to think of it, I don't really like the idea a runnin' with 'em either, especially not now, but if I was pushed just a little more I might run with 'em just the same. Weird. I think this and then somethin' deep down in me says, "No ya wouldn't." And that little voice is sure as can be.

Anyway, Pop, he's funny, but he does have a way a turnin' the knife now and then. "Heard them scamps drivin' around town last night. They stop here?"

"Just a sec, Pop."

Big Ol' is on the phone.

"Hey, Dale. There's a wreck out on 28. Car carrier lost his trailer and a bunch of cars got loose. Nobody hurt but the road's blocked. Wreckers comin' from Newberry too. We gotta get them cars off the road. I'll come by with the wrecker, we'll go out together. The old man's gonna hold down the garage 'till we get back."

"Shoot, I got a paintin' job today over at Brown's, but it's gonna rain anyway. Okay, I'll be ready."

"Yup. Good. Later."

"What's that?" Pop says.

"Car carrier lost its load out on the highway."

Pop whistles. "That'll be a mess."

"That's what Big Ol' said."

"Anyway though, did them scamps stop by here?"

"Well, they slowed down and yelled, but when I didn't come out they went away."

Pop looks at me kinda funny, maybe tryin' to figure out if what I'm sayin' is true, too. I see him kinda glance at Carrie. Them two got a tough row ta hoe with me. Finally he says, "Must be turnin' over a new leaf. Or maybe they figured out somebody else has." Pop pats me on the back. That feels good. My Dad thinks I'm okay. I don't say nothin', but we kinda look at each other.

"I come over to see if them two rascals of yours wanta pick berries with their gramps."

"Want and will are two different things," Carrie says grinnin'. "I'll get'em up."

Carrie goes on out and upstairs. I hear her talkin' to the kids. I sip some coffee then go and get Pop some.

"Have a good talk with Father?" Pop says after a minute.

Everybody knows everything in this town, but I don't mind.

"More work than talk, but yeah, I'd say so."

"That's good. And I hear the boy's comin' tomorrow."

I smile. "Yup."

"Well, that's fine. Just fine. Like the Prodigal, eh? Wonder how he's lookin'."

"Everybody seems to wonder that. Guess he probably looks kinda rough and crotchety, like his gramps."

"Oh...one with the jokes this mornin' are ya?" Pop slaps

me harder on the back. Just hard enough to hurt. It's a good, good moment. And we just sit there quiet.

Pretty soon Big Ol' pulls up out front with the wrecker and I find my hat and gloves and wallet and head out, just as the kids come wanderin' down the stairs. Carrie runs over and plants a quick kiss on me and I hear Pop say, "Well who are these little bears rollin' outta the den?" just as I go out.

When I get out to the wrecker, Big Ol' is sippin' his coffee and looks serious. I walk around and get in on the passenger side.

He looks over at me. "That damned Hughie came to see me to bitch about you last night. Woke up the wife. She was mad as hell."

"Drunk?"

"Stinkin', but he was kinda funny. Like he couldn't figure you out. Guess he pushed all the buttons he usually does and you wouldn't give him what he wanted."

"Guess that's about right… Sorry."

"What the hell are you sorry for? Ain't your fault Hughie's a fuckin' asshole."

"Sometimes, he is I guess."

"You defendin' him?"

"Hell no. Just sometimes, he's okay."

"I guess."

"Well, we're gonna be busy this mornin'."

"Sounds like."

I call over to Browns and tell 'em what's goin' on. Tell 'em I'll be over later if it don't rain. They're a nice old couple. No hassles. They're more worried about the mess on the road. That was easy. Can't believe I used to leave folks like them hangin' just 'cause I liked to run with the Pups. Ain't right. Never was. Your conscience is a funny thing. When I was doin' bad I didn't feel nothin'. Now that I ain't, I feel terrible about what I done before.

We don't say much most of the way out to the accident. Both thinkin' things over, how it's gonna be. I'm thinkin' about Ike too, and Hughie, and Father and Pop and Carrie and the kids. Too much really. Not used to it. It's a kinda relief when we get to the wreck.

The highway is a mess. So, so lucky nobody was hurt. Hitch just snapped and the safety hitches held on, but the driver was goin' along about 75, and they just started swingin' before he could get it all stopped, the cars broke loose of the couplings, spilled out, couple of 'em hit each other, then the trailer rolled. Well…like I said. A mess.

We start haulin' what we can to a dealership in Newberry. Couple have to go on a flatbed straight to the junk yard. Insurance people there. Cops tryin' to get the road clean. One trooper is Teddy Grace. Nice fella. Picked me up once when I spent a night in the jug. He always liked me for some reason. Wasn't much reason to right at that point. He's a big fella, almost the size of Big Ol' but not a ounce a fat, about my age. He was a Marine too. That might be why he likes me.

"Dale! You're lookin' good. Good to see you're gainfully employed."

"Oh ya. Gotta make ends meet, you know?"

"Sure, sure. What a mess, huh?"

"Nobody hurt, though, that's the good part."

"Sure. When it's just metal it isn't quite so… How's the wife and kids?"

"Oh, good good. Growin' like weeds. Yer's?"

"Oh same. One's off to college now. Michigan! Scholarship for micro-biology."

"What's…that?"

"Ha…damned if I know, Dale!"

We have a good laugh over that one while the flat bed boys are loadin' up a new pick up, well, it was new, that's blockin' the way of our next one that we can hitch.

"Seein' any of your buddies? Whatdaya call 'em, 'The Pups'?"

"Little as possible, Ted." I look at him kinda serious. "Just got back with the wife. Tryin' to keep it that way."

"Oh…runnin' with those boys wouldn't help that much I guess."

I nod a little.

"Well...that's good, Dale. That's damned good. Good for you. Keep it up. Us Marines gotta keep up the reputation you know." He winks at me. This feels good. This feels good just be part of what...the community I guess. People feelin' good about me. People pullin' for me.

Ya. This is good. Maybe, when he comes back I can make Ike feel this way too. Least I can do. Ma says that there's no reason not to be nice to everybody, even if they're mean. What can it hurt? Ya know? What can it hurt?

It's 2 o'clock or so before all our runs to Newberry and wherever are done. Big Ol' and me are havin' a coupla orange sodas in the truck on our way back to the garage.

"Look at the two of us," Big Ol' says.

"Ha, right? You don't have to drink pop for me, Rex."

"Well, been watchin' you the last couple days and I'm thinkin' maybe it's the way to go for me too."

"Whatever works."

"So, the boy comes home this week, eh?"

"Tomorrow."

"Well, that's somethin'. Everybody in town talkin' about it."

"No surprise there. When ain't they talkin'?"

He laughs. "True enough. Well. Good luck with that. I'll try to manage the Pups for ya."

"Appreciate that, Rex."

"Well, they don't mean no harm, Dale."

"Oh I know, but that don't stop 'em from doin' it."

He looks away, nods over the wheel out towards the highway. "That's true enough."

Right about then the rain cuts loose. I call over to Browns again. Looks like good weather the next two days, but I explain about Ike comin' home tomorrow and they are on board right away. We decide I'll give her another try next Monday. They're gonna be gone on the weekend anyway, so we'll only lose a few days. Nice, nice folks.

When I get home Carrie is asleep. No jobs for me. That might not be good. Rain pourin' down. I'm just gettin' antsy, ain't never been good at sittin' still. Just about then door on the screen porch flies open and Pop and the kids come in with buckets of blueberries.

I walk out to the porch and the three of 'em come in just drenched all smilin'. I don't even care. They're like...what...like if you drew a picture of happiness, this is what it would look like. Seems that way to me anyway. It makes me glad, ya know? Just glad. Here's my dad and my kids and they're havin' a good time and now they're wet and it's like...so lively, ya know? I'm part of it just standin' here grinnin' with 'em. I seen a lot a bad stuff in my life, so that makes this sweeter. Ya don't have to look around to be happy, I guess. You just have to look right in front of ya and not be so picky.

"A old man with a long white beard in a great big wooden cabin boat went by while we was pickin'. Asked if we seen any stray animals goin' around two by two!" Pop says and he's just laughin'.

"Name of Noah?" I ask and the kids get it, then. Well, I think Kelly already got it with what Pop said, and we're all laughin'.

All the commotion wakes Carrie up and she's comin' down the stairs lookin' sleepy.

"Oh Care, you didn't need..."

She waves me off and finds some raggedy old towels and takes them out to the porch. She blocks Donny from comin' in about four times and just keeps pointin' to the towels. He ain't gettin' it right away, or is havin' fun pretendin' like he ain't, anyway. It's a funny little cat and mouse game and I can't help laughin', until Carrie gives me a hard look. Then turns it into a grin. It's all good. Just so good, ya know?

She takes the three buckets of berries, "Oh Pop, these look prime!" she says.

"Ya, they're big this year."

"I'll have to make some blueberry pie and crumble."

"Will ya have any for a back achin' old man?"

"Oh, we might, we might." Carrie shoots Pop that smile she keeps just for him. They been in on it together for a long time.

Tryin' to keep the family together, tryin' to keep me goin' in a straight line. Tryin' to make everything as good as they can for everybody they love. Damned if they don't do it most of the time. Time for me to start pullin' my weight along them lines. I decide right then, like I been doin' the last couple days, I guess, that I'm gonna do my bit. Decidin' and doin' are two different things, but I feel pretty determined. Right now any reason not to do what I can for all these folks is just gettin'…what… drowned out by all this good around me. How in hell can I do anything else? Why would I? A guy would have to be nuts, ya know? How can anything else be even close to this good? Just have to lock it in. Always remember it. I ain't been so good at that in the past, but I'm going to try real hard to remember what I got ridin' on this. I'm gonna make it all true and good for as long as I can, for Carrie and the kids, and Pop and Ma and for Father Bill and Big Ol', and maybe, in some ways even for Hughie and the Pups.

Wouldn't ya know it? Right then the phone rings. For a second I get a bad feelin', but it's Ma and she wants ta know where Pop is.

"He's right here, Ma."

"He didn't take his phone with him again."

"Didn't know he had one."

"Well, he does, and he won't use it. He okay? Crazy old man out in the wet with those kids?"

"He's fine. Wanna talk to him?"

"No, just tell him to get home when he's done bothering you."

"He's just fine, Ma. Want me to come over and get you so you can join the fun?"

"No, no. Lots of work to do here. Good to have some peace. Just checking to see if the old man is okay."

"Well, he is."

"Okay. Dale?"

"Ya Ma?"

"How are you?"

I know what that means. "I'm fine, Ma. Just great really."

"Stay between the lines. Talk to Father Bill if you need to. He's a very good, man, Dale. I don't always agree with him, but he's a very good, man."

"Ya, I think so too."

"Like I say, call him when things feel bad. He's the best around for helping that, I think."

"You bet, Ma."

"Okay, love you all."

"Love ya back, Ma."

Pop looks at me. It's even kind of a serious look for once. They musta really had a blowout about that phone. That kinda makes me happy. Good to know even they have dustups sometimes. Makes me feel a little better about me.

He says, "She's on about that blasted phone I bet."

"A little, just worried I think.

"She'll worry ya ta death." He winks at me.

"She wants ya to come home."

"Oh, not so fast. I better let her cool off them jets of hers."

"Got some coffee on," Carrie calls from the other room.

"Ah, just right." Pop says.

We head on into the kitchen.

Now, Pop never says stuff straight out. He ain't never tryin' to be mean; he ain't never tryin' to have somethin' over on ya, he just don't like to bug people. He does his best not to. So I know it's somethin' big when he says:

"So, had the police scanner on, when I was in the truck with the kids."

Carrie says, "Uh oh. Another wreck?"

"Well, course that stuff out on the highway was all over it, but there was somethin' else."

I get a bad feelin'. I say, "C'mon Pop, out with it. It's somethin' I need to know ain't it?"

"Depends."

Carrie says, "On what?" Now she's listen' close.

Pop sighs a little, looks around to see the kids aren't there. "Looks like the Pups got picked up over in the Soo. Looks like they give a customs officer a bad time when he wouldn't let them cross… Chatter on the radio was about them gettin' turned over to the local boys."

There ain't much you can do worse than mess with a customs officer at the border to Canada. You get in a scuffle and take a pop at a village cop, or even a state cop, you're in enough trouble. But you take a swing at a customs officer anywhere, even just at the international bridge across the St. Mary's River to Canada, well, you're askin' for…what's it…a international incident. They're gonna throw away the key.

"Oh Jese…Goin' over to the strip club probably."

Carrie shoots me a look, turns back towards the stove.

That slipped, but no point in tryin' to pretend I ain't been there. I think for a second. "They was here around midnight. Even if they'd got over there, they wouldn'ta had more 'n fifteen minutes before that club closed. Idiots."

"Figured you'd find out even if I didn't tell ya."

"Ya. Ya, yer right, Pop. Thanks."

"What's more, looks like they're still lookin' for one of your friends. Couldn't make it out completely."

My phone rings. Carrie shoots me another look. I don't need to tell you what it means. If I go anywhere to help the Pups there will be hell to pay. I don't blame her one bit. I don't know quite what to do. I answer the phone. Naturally it's Big Ol'.

"You hear?"

"Pop just told me."

"Fella with the stun gun is in the hospital with a skull fracture. Looks like it's Shine that done it. Doctors say the customs guy will make it, thank God. But, well…they beat up a cop, Dale. Nobody's gonna go easy on'em now. They've used up their chances. What's worse, Shine's still…at large. Drove off in the chevy and left Hughie and Chessy to clean up what's mostly his mess. He'll be lucky if he don't wind up dead. Nobody's gonna think this is just small town shenanigans, like the other times."

"Oh…no, I guess not. "

"Now before you do anything, Dale, I'm just gonna say it.

This ain't your fault. This ain't your lookout. If you'd a been with them, it would be even worse. You couldn't a stopped'em. You'd be up to your neck with'em. Hell, this might even be a good thing for you. Dale, them guys been headed this way long as you and me can remember. Ya, they're our friends, but we didn't make'em do this. And no matter what they done for us in the past…none a that matters. You listenin'?"

"Yeah, but you're goin' over to the Soo to check on'em ain't ya?"

"Well…ya, Dale I am. Maybe I shouldn't. But you ain't goin' with me! Your boy's comin' home. You just got back with the wife. I'm bettin' she's probably lookin' at ya pretty hard right now."

She is of course.

"Now you listen to that look, Dale. She's right. I know you and Hughie go back farther than any a us, but that don't mean squat. She's more important. Your kids are more important. Just let me go over there and see how bad it is. I got nothin' to lose by just checkin' in. I'll send your regards…ya know…explain it to'em. I'll keep ya posted. Maybe you can help, even, without comin' over there. But stay away. Oh and watch out for that fuckin' Shine. He shows up. Call a cop. Call Teddy Grace."

"Ya. Okay. Ya, I can see all that…" That's what I say but my conscience is just gnawin' at me. "Okay, Rex. Let me know…if there's anything…"

"There's nothin' for you to do, Dale. Stay the hell away. You hear me?"

"…Yup. Thanks."

"Nothin' to thank me for." He hangs up.

Pop, seein' Carrie and me need to talk, gets up and says, "Well, enjoy them berries."

Carrie says, "Oh, we will! Thanks for entertaining the rug rats."

"Hey, watch what ya call my grandkids!" He winks and laughs.

They laugh together. Pop goes out.

I can just imagine what Carrie's gonna say as soon as he's

out the door.

When he's gone she comes back in, looks at me real calm.

"Call Father Bill."

That, I don't expect.

"Call Father Bill right now…"

"I'm okay."

"No you're not. I can see that vague look in your eye. And your stomach hurts doesn't it?"

It does. Damn she knows me.

"Call Father Bill." She turns back to the stove.

I call Father Bill and Carrie takes me out to meet him by St. Brigids at the lake. Then she pulls away, headed back to the house. It doesn't come into my head until later that she drove me to keep me from going to the Soo. She figures worst that can happen is Father will take me there. That's good thinkin'. But I keep thinkin', what if that fuckin' Shine shows up at the house? Well, I guess Carrie can handle Shine and ten more like him. Especially if he's sober.

Father's sittin' on a bench down by the lake in between the outdoor stations of the cross they got there. He's readin' a book. I read the name and it's this Merton fella again. Weird title: Zen and the Birds of Appetite. Somethin' I noticed. Smart people read books with funny titles.

Father Bill don't look up when I get close.

"What do you want to do?" he says.

"Huh?"

"What do you want to do?" He looks up at me from where he's sittin', those big bushy white eyebrows all pulled down over his eyes, and them dark eyes just flashin'. He's givin' me a look like I'm supposed to understand, like he knows I do understand, but I don't think I do. But later, I can see he's right. I do get it. I don't never give myself enough credit. How do all these folks know more about me than I do?

"Free will. You've got one," he says.

"I don't…"

He looks down, kind of rubs at his chin whiskers, then says lookin' out at the lake. "You're free to do anything you want to do.

What do you want to do?"

I think about that for a long time. "I wanna help my friends, but not make Carrie mad, and not get so messed up with the Pups that I end up missin' Ike when he comes."

"Can you do all that?"

"I don't think so."

"Why not?"

"Well, there's consequences."

He looks up and grins at me. His face is softer now, like a friend that knows you good and likes you. "You're a philosopher, Dale."

I laugh. "I'm just a beat up vet."

"The best kind. Tell me about the consequences."

"Well…" I look down and my hands are shakin'. I can feel my feet on the wet ground and if I force myself I can see the lake, and father lookin' like he's waitin' kind of checkin' me out readin' every little move…But in another way, a big way, I'm back at that roadside in Afghanistan and that kid is screamin' and blood is everywhere, and all them dark eyes are around us, lookin' at us and guns are pointed outwards in a circle around us and past that circle of guardsmen, weekend warriors scared as shit, like I say, all them dark eyes and turbans and words don't none of us but the interpreters understand…

"Stay with me, Dale."

"Well…I want…"

"A drink."

I look at him and he's stopped smilin'…

"A bunch of 'em really."

"Me too." It's not a joke. He ain't laughin'.

"Father, I don't see how that helps, talkin'…"

"We help each other. We don't give in when something like a a drink looks like an easy solution, looks too good to be true, because it always is. Right now it probably seems like the Christian thing to do is to go and help your friends, right?"

I nod.

"But like you say, there are consequences."

"Yeah."

"Okay, now, back to it. What are they? The consequences, I mean."

I think for a second. It helps to sort things out. How do folks know what you need before you do? There's lots of folks in the world way smarter than me, I guess. I just go from one moment to the next. It's like checkers. I never see the next move comin', folks like Father Bill, and Carrie, and even Ma and Pop seem to see it all comin' down the line. I don't know how that works. Finally, I get at it. "If I help the pups, everybody will be mad…"

"Including…"

"Carrie, Ma, Pop, though he won't say nothin' about it, Kelly, and in his little way even Donny…and…well…you."

"Wrong."

"W-what?"

"None of those folks will be mad."

"Sure they…"

"They'll be disappointed."

"Oh…"

"They'll be surprised and sad that you didn't do better, that you didn't make the right choice."

"What's the right choice?"

"The hard one."

"Either way it's a hard one. The Pups'll be disappointed just like…"

"No they won't."

"Sure they…"

"No, they won't be disappointed. They'll be mad."

"I don't get…"

"They'll be MAD that you didn't help them out of their sorry ass problem. They'll blame it on you and they'll be 100% wrong to blame you. They're not really disappointed in you as a person, the way a parent or somebody who really loves you would be. It doesn't hurt them more than it hurts you. They're just selfish. And I know that's judgmental, and I hate to be that way, because I've got plenty of my own sins to reckon with, but it's the unvarnished truth. They're just selfish. They're mad because it's going to affect them, not disappointed about what's happening to you and your morality, judging from the fact that you're not standing by them. And, in fact, by not going there, you are standing by them. You're forcing them to be better people. But, true disappointment born out of a lifetime of love… No, Dale, they don't care enough about you for that… Even though you, the best person of the bunch by far, will naturally think so."

"But Hughie…"

"You've known him a long time."

"Yeah."

"Okay, so, does he love you?"

"Well…" I turn all red. "I guess…guess so."

"What is that love based on?"

"Well, we been through so much together."

"Like what?"

"Well, well all the stuff on the playground in school and lots of hunting trips and well, drinkin', fishin', lots of scrapes…" I smile a little bit.

"What has Hughie done to show that he loves you?"

"Well…he saved me once." He did, but all of a sudden, seems like there's more, other ways maybe Hughie cares about me. Can't put my finger on it.

"Really? He saved you?" Father seems surprised. "Okay. Tell me about that. This wasn't in the service was it?"

"Oh no, Hughie was never with me in the service. He was out on the boats in the Gulf. He'd never a made the Marines."

Father kinda gestures for me to go on. His face is all… well…intense, under them white eyebrows.

"Well, in first grade, there was this girl on the playground who was beatin' the crap outta me and well…he pulled her off."

I can see Father tryin' not to laugh.

"Well…she was a pretty big girl," I say.

I can't help grinnin' and then I break a little…and he just loses it, and then I join in laughin' and we're sittin' there laughin' like little boys laughin' at a fart joke. That goes on for a long time and starts up a time or two again and then, finally, finally we're done. And oh, does it ever feel good. So alive, you know? Just part of what's goin' on right now…I don't know…I don't know how to put it.

"Okay…ha…okay Dale. Put that one incident…" he almost breaks again but stops, "…put him saving you from the wrath of a little girl on the playground a million years ago, up against the ways that Carrie and your Ma and Pop show they love you every day. The way your kids show you. Are they equal?"

I think for a long time. It isn't just that one thing, Hughie did for me. But Father's right, it isn't the same as the way my family cares, but there is somethin' that's more than just…I don't know… drinkin' buddies. But I say what Father wants to hear, what is really true, mostly.

"No. No way. Not close really."

"So…"

"But Father…Hughie needs me. And…well…he don't know how to help himself."

Father looks away for a second. "You're a good person, Dale."

"That ain't…"

"No, dammit!" Father shoots me a look that shuts me right up. It's real. Here's the real man, under that collar, I think. "Listen to me. You are a good person. You are wiling to take yourself into hell, and make no mistake that's just what it would be… Losing Carrie again, missing Ike's visit, Kelly and Donny and your mother and dad giving you the looks they would give you and all of that for the sake of a low life friend." I open my mouth for a second and Father shoots that look again. "Don't defend, him, you know I'm right! He's a guy who, even though he may say and think it isn't true, is only looking out for himself. You're willing to take yourself into hell for a friend who really, really, Dale, is far from worth that sacrifice. That is as Christian as it can be."

I was with him for a while, but now Father's really confused me. "But…I don't get it…you don't want me to do that…help Hughie…right?"

"Right. For your own sake, and the sake of your family, don't try to bail Hughie out or help him in any other way, even though it's probably the most Christian thing to do."

"That's confusin'."

He smiles at me. "That's how you know you're on the right track, Dale. Still want a drink?"

"Yeah."

"Okay, let's go over to your house together, and stick together until we're both sure we aren't going to have one."

So, twenty minutes later I show back up at the house and I see Carrie at the back door opening it, smiling. Probably breathed a sigh of relief for five minutes when she saw us pull into the driveway.

"Hello, Father." She says, her eyes on the edge of tears. "Stay for dinner?"

"Fish?"

"You bet."

"How can a priest turn that down?"

So, he stays. And really, we have a fine, fine time. One of the very best I can remember. The kids laughin', Father just bein' a fella, Carrie beamin' from ear to ear, just the best thing of all. We sit out on the screen porch after, all full a fish. The kids bein' silly, Father tellin' jokes and teasin' 'em. I can hear Carrie movin' around the house. Great night.

Then the phone rings. It's Big Ol'.

"Hello."

"Put Father on. He's with ya, right?"

"How do you…"

"Never mind. Put him on. This ain't got nothin' to do with you."

"Oh…okay…"

I hand Father the phone. He gives me kind of a funny look.

"Hello?" he says. I'm wonderin' what's comin' next because really Rex ain't even Catholic and don't hardly know Father from Adam.

"That's a wonderful idea…Rex. Yes. Yes. He's fine." He

winks at me. "I think Carrie can handle any nonsense he's got in store. Yes. Yes. Oh…I know the address. Yes. Been there a time or two before. Wish I hadn't. See you…" He looks at his watch. "…in about an hour and a half. Don't you take any guff from them either, Rex. Okay. God bless. Goodbye."

I look at Father. He smiles and sighs. "Well, it's probably better not to, but I guess I have to tell you. Rex wants me to come and talk to Hughie and Chessy. See if I can't get them to leave you alone. I hate to leave, but I think it's the right thing. Now, you two watch out for that other one…"

"Shine?" I say.

"Yes. As I understand it, he's the one who actually hurt the officer. Don't know that I've ever met him."

I manage to get out a little kinda grim smile, "You ain't missed much. Look, Father, I really think I should come with…"

Father just shakes his head. "Not on my watch, Dale."

That makes me feel terrible, but Father heads me off. "Dale Sylvanus, this is not your fault. This is the job I do, the job I chose, the job I love most of the time. Let me do it and you stay the hell out of it!" The kids are staring at him.

"Oops! I'll have to say a few more Our Father's for that one. He winks at me."

Donny says, "Maybe a Hail Mary too!"

Everybody laughs, especially Father.

Carrie walks in about then. "What's so funny?"

"Long story. I'll fill you in on our walk out to my car." He shoots a pretty stern look at Carrie for half a second, then smiles. "You don't mind a walk in the moonlight with an old priest do you?

"Father!" Donny says, and Carrie breaks out laughing.

Carrie's quick. She picks up on it all without even glancing at me.

A second later they're gone, and I hear my truck start up. I wonder for a second why my truck, and then I figure it out. I won't leave in Carrie's car, or Father's, especially since the keys are probably hidden. I can't find a place in me that's mad at either one of them. It's good to be loved.

Then Carrie comes back in.

"Well, Ike's coming back tomorrow family. Let's hit the hay!"

The kids are pretty upset to be goin' to bed at 9, but Carrie works them into it, and off they go.

We sit down on the porch for a good long spell, talkin' things over, practical like. Where are Ike and his girl...his wife, and daughter...gonna sleep...stuff like that. Then we talk about bigger stuff. Stuff we've already talked about, but need to go over again. What to say, what not to say. All that. What we don't talk about at all is Hughie and the Pups. But my head's on a bit of a swivel all the time. What am I gonna do if Shine shows up? But after while, even that worry goes away. It's good, so good, just to be here with Carrie.

We're sittin' there 'till after dark just talkin'. Then my phone rings. And Carrie's right away tense, but it ain't Big Ol' or Father or Shine, it's a service call; with Big Ol' gone they come straight to me. That same old woman with the flat from yesterday, on her way through again, she's got another flat, again out on the highway. It's a different tire she says. Either the tires wore out at the same time, or she keeps runnin' over somethin' in her driveway or somewhere she always goes, I'm thinkin'. Either that or she's one a them people who just is lonely and wants to yell at somebody.

"Be right there." I says. I have to be. Rex is gone. Nobody else in town. Can't leave a poor ol' lady alone at night on a highway.

"What..." Carrie starts.

I tell her.

Then she says, with a look on her face that says I'd better not say nothin', "I'm going with you."

"Oh...Carrie..."

She don't even waiver.

I sigh. "Okay, never been on a service call with ya before."

She smiles. Might be fun. "I'll go tell Kelly. I'll offer her some babysitting money. Sure she's up on her cell phone anyway."

"Don't you make 'em leave them things down here?"

"You didn't hear the noise on the stairs a while ago?" After a second I get it. Kelly musta come down, got the phone, probably so she could talk to the Chesterfield boy.

I smile at her. "You're a good Mom."

She smiles. "The best." Then she laughs. "I hope so, Dale."

"You are."

It's rainin' hard when we pull out on the road. And sure enough, just down the way, right across from the corner street light, between the wiper blades, I can see the old lady from yesterday's little car by the side a the road. I can see the relief on Carrie's face too that there's really a old lady to help. I don't blame her for doubtin' me.

Well, I have the tire fixed in a flash really. She already got the other one patched and I put it back on for a spare. I remember to switch off my headlamp before I go up to her window, 'cause I don't need to give her anything extra to squawk about. I tell her she should get a couple new tires ASAP. She kinda…what…scowls at me, says, "Well, isn't that just like. You just see me coming don't you?"

I smile at her through the rain. I give her Big Ol's card and it has some grease on it and she gives me a bad look. I try not to laugh. She rolls up her window and I can tell she can't see much and I almost tell her to wait out the rain, but I figure she'll just holler at me. Which she would. So, just as soon as she gets her window down, she pulls out not able to see much I'm sure.

It's like a bad dream when I see the other car.

The driver's in a hurry, roarin' from the west, and I say out loud "No!" but it's way too late when the driver ditches his brand new Toyota on the far side of the road to avoid hittin' her and she never even sees him and just keeps headin' east and the Toyota flips over across the road under the street light, not far from the corner into Hunter, and it's upside down in the ditch that's overflowin' with water and I start runnin' over there, and first thing I know Carrie's right next to me.

"You've got to get them out. I can't help them if you don't get them out." Her voice is calm as can be. Nurse's voice.

I get to the car and wade into the ditch and turn on my

headlamp. I can see pretty good between that and the street light. The Toyota is kinda tilted up towards me but upside-down and it's banged up pretty good and the door is pinned under the water, but I can see through the passenger side that there's a woman strapped in upside down and screamin'. I got the tire iron in my hand and I yell, "Cover your eyes!"

But she's shouting in some language I don't understand, but that seems almost familiar, so I just go ahead with the smashin' once, twice, three times and the window finally gives and then I can hear her and she's just terrified, but I still don't understand what she's sayin'. It's weird, but I know she's speakin' Farsi, from hearin' it all the time in the desert. I don't have time to wonder about it or to flash on that roadside in Afghanistan, I just undo her seatbelt, drag her out, and I notice…funny what ya notice…she's real pregnant, and Carrie's got her and the woman, girl really, keeps babblin' and I look into the car and finally she says in English, "My baby!"

Then, "Oh…oh…my husband!"

So I reach down in the water across to the driver's seat and there is somebody else, of course somebody had to be drivin', and he's completely under water and he's out cold. So I stick my head down under water and unhitch him and wrench my back good pullin' him out. He's a big fella with long hair tied back and a red beard and somethin' half occurs to me, but before I can make it out complete Carrie takes hold of him and together we pull him out onto the grass.

And then, when Carrie says it, I know what was workin' in my head a second before. She says it kinda quiet like she's talkin' with somebody else's voice.

"Oh, my Isaac. Little Ike." she says.

And the girl is just shrieking in Farsi, between saying, "My baby, my baby!"

"Broken leg." Carrie is saying now. "Some contusions. Probable concussion." And I wonder why she's tellin' me this and I look over and see she's on the phone. "Yup, and a woman as well, no apparent major injuries. A few minor cuts. Possible concussion. Hard to say. Middle Eastern, can't make out everything she's saying.

Dale, get to work on your son. He needs CPR. I check the heart and it's beatin' strong, but he ain't breathin' so I start mouth to mouth and right off he spits out a bunch of god awful water, and comes around.

Now the woman is screamin', "My baby! My baby!"

Carrie says real calm, "Honey, I can see you're pregnant; I'm a nurse. Your husband is awake. It's going to be okay."

And all of a sudden Ike, my son, comes around completely and says, "No, she means Dorri! Our little...our little girl! She's in the back seat. He tries to get up and crawl back into the car but grabs his leg and screams, and just for a second, just long enough, I hear that fella screamin' by the road in Afghanistan. Then I come back when Ike says, "Dad, Pop! You gotta get my girl outta there!"

Jesus Christ Almighty! This is my boy, I think, and his family! My family!

Carrie's still calm, "Dale, get the little girl." She sucks back a sob. "Get our grandchild out of there!"

So I stick my head and shoulders back in there and get into what must be the back seat. Can't tell, dark as midnight, my headlamp is out, and I just start reachin'. I feel a body and have a hell of a time with the carseat and my air's startin' to run out, but it's weird, a little voice says, "Get your grandchild out." And it ain't Carrie. And I ain't thinkin' of nothin' else. And I get hold of that car seat and I use every ounce of strength I got and a bunch more from the adrenaline that's pumpin' through me, and I just tear the damned thing loose and I pull that little girl out still in it and Carrie's got her and the next thing I know I'm gaspin' and spittin' and sputterin' Carrie's sayin' still calm, "I gotta get her heart going. Look after them!"

I can't see nothin' and I start to pass out.

"Stay with me, Dale, damn you!"

And then I hear the screamin' comin' from both Ike and his wife and I start movin' from one to the other.

Ike says, "Dad, just help them! I'll be okay."

So I move over to the woman and she's still spittin' and sputterin' in Farsi and then every once in a while, "My baby, save my baby!" And her eyes are kinda rollin' back in her head, and I'm thinkin', she's goin' into shock.

"Dale? You with me?" I can see she's already seen what I see.

"Ya, Care. Ya, I'm good."

"Okay, good. Come over here and start mouth to mouth on the girl; I've got her heart going."

We switch quick and I start in on it. And that voice is there again. "Give her life. Get her back."

Then Carrie's back on the phone, "Five minutes? Jesus, hurry! I've got the woman calmed down, but I think there's some shock…Ike? Ike, honey, stay with me…He's out."

So, by now I'm well into the mouth to mouth on the little girl. My granddaughter. And I start to panic a little because nothin's happenin' and I'm gettin' dizzy again, and then all of a sudden, all of a sudden she spits and sputters and pukes up a bunch of water and starts cryin' but I'm hearin' more cryin' too. And just for a second I flash on all my little babies cryin', Ike, and Kelly, and Donny, their first cries and their last cries and it's all kinda mixin' together with this little girl's cries.

Carrie says, cryin' too, just as the ambulance pulls up, "Ike. Ike. Oh, good, good you're with me. You're with me. Your daughter's fine, honey. Your pop's got her. She's just fine. And your wife's fine."

"The baby too?" he says.

"Yeah, hon. The baby too. I'm positive. The ambulance is here. I'll ride with you all."

And I hold the little girl tight to keep her quiet and she's so, so pretty. So… what?…precious.

And I look up and see the stars are out, and I notice it ain't rainin' anymore.

Wednesday, 7:01 a.m.

During the night there's a lot of things to get through my head: Carrie and me are grandparents; we've been grandparents for four years, and now in two months or so, we're gonna be again because that baby is just fine; our Isaac, Ike, is doing fine too, has a beard, is making pots for a lot of money near Portland, Oregon; he's married to a beautiful woman named Donya, who is from, wouldn't ya know it the way life is lately? from Afghanistan. She's a college teacher, out in Portland, from a rich family who are smart people too, and her parents love Ike, and don't have no problem with his being white, and Christian, or that he didn't go to college neither, I guess. What's more, and outta all the things that's happened you might think this wouldn't be too surprisin', but really it surprises me more than anything else: Ike loves me. What's more, ain't never been angry at me. Well, not for anything I didn't deserve, at least. Everybody is going to be okay, what's more, everybody in their little family, including Donya's parents, "Abbasi" I think the name is, who talked to me in tears by phone from Oregon, thinks Carrie and me are heroes. Life is good. How the hell did this happen so sudden?

At about a quarter to seven the phone starts ringin' again. The first call is from Jen Hicks. She wants to know, will I make a statement for her.

"A statement…"

" For the paper. About what happened."

"About…oh geez…what did the Puppies do now? Is Father okay? Did…did they catch Shine?"

"What…?"

"The…the…Puppies…ain't that what you're calling about?"

"No! No. Dale, don't you know that you're a hero? You and Carrie?"

"Oh…oh…that. Well, it's just what you do."

"Just what…Dale, you saved three people…four people… from…"

"Carrie did more saving than I did. Why don't you talk to her? Here I'll…"

"Oh, oh, I will. Of course, but the angle, the angle is that… well…here you are a guy who works, well, works with his hands for a living, who isn't in the business of saving lives like Carrie, and you save four people and they turn out to be your estranged family. What's more, you're a Gulf war vet, and they're…well… Muslims."

"The angle?" I'm way behind her. "What? 'Strange'?"

"You know, how the media is going to shape it?"

"I don't know what you're…"

"Dale, come on, just tell me how it happened."

"Oh, well, Jen, it wasn't really….Look let me give you to Carrie."

Jen is still talkin' but I real quick hand over the phone and Carrie talks to her for a little bit, says that maybe later today we'll sit down with her and give her a nice little story but right now we just want to be with the family. While Carrie's sayin' all this, her phone goes off. She sets up a time with Jen, picks up the phone, gets a funny look on her face after saying hello and then says, "No comment." She shuts off her phone and mine goes off again.

"Hello."

"Mr. Sylvanus?"

"Yes."

"This is Brian Tesch from CBS News This Morning…."

"This is who?…" I look over and I see Carrie, and she grabs the phone from me.

"No comment," she says, and shuts it down too.

I look at her. "Care, what the hell is…"

She grins a little, then shakes her head and puts her arms around me. "Dale, we're the story of the day, in this town. Maybe in this state." She laughs. "Maybe in the whole country. Like it or not."

"What? Why?"

"The angle…" Carrie looks thoughtful. "Like Jen said. I don't think we better talk to anybody but her until we sort this out."

And the calls keep comin'. Now that our phones are shut

down, calls start comin' in on the hospital phones, on the phones the doctors and nurses got, even on Ike's phone that's somehow okay. it was zipped into the pancho he had on. It's sittin' on his bed stand as he lies there sleeping in the hospital bed. We took the call from the Abassies on it. Donya's phone didn't make it.

I pick it up, when Carrie is out of the room and answer. I don't know why. Curious, I guess. "Hello."

"Good morning! Mr. Isaac Sylvanus? Hope you're doing well this morning, could you tell me about last night? This is Jeff Nicholas from CNN."

I hang up. Unbelievable. Like something out of a dream.

"Okay, who was that?" Carrie is frowning when she comes back in.

"CNN."

"Wow…" She suddenly smiles. "The baby, Doc says, is just thriving! I knew it was. I was worried after I told Donya the baby was fine last night, but Doc says it's very very strong. No reason at all for it not to get to full term. And, it's a boy! Donya doesn't mind us all knowing. She's so happy! Sweet girl."

"How is…the mother."

Carrie shoots me a sharp look. "She's your daughter-in-law, Dale. And her name is Donya."

"Nice name."

Carrie looks around, then leans in and whispers. "Where are you on this, Dale? Tell me honestly. I know what you've said…" she looks around again "…in the past, when you came back from the war those times, about how…people from the Mideast.. and they're all the same and you can't trust any of them especially the women…"

"That…that was Marine talk. That was just stupid things you say when you're in battle or when you're out and you're trying to make yourself big…you know with the guys."

"Yeah? Sure. But do you really believe any of it? Is even one percent of one percent of that what you really think is true?"

I really do have to think for a minute, "one percent of one percent…" and I surprise myself.

Carrie giggles a little, looking at my face.

"You have the most amazing smile when you don't know it, Dale."

I look up at her and I feel…new.

"You know, Care…I really don't. I don't think any of that, not any of that. Not anymore."

"Since when?"

"Since…I don't know…not just since last night. Since…" I can't place it. Was it when I swore off the booze? Was it when Father Bill started talking to me? Was it when Ike called me? Was it before that?

"I don't know…but it's been a while. I…I just didn't know. Maybe…maybe it was when I was out at the River House a couple weeks back…no…hell…that was a year ago, with the Pups and Shine started goin' on and on about Mexicans, and everyone taking our jobs, and I remember thinking 'When the hell have you ever even looked for a job?' and I was thinkin' how stupid Shine is and don't even know it and I was thinkin' how stupid it is to think a way about people you don't hardly know. Then I got thinkin' I had the right to have a opinion because I'd been to Iraq and Afghanistan, then I started thinkin' though, how much time when I wasn't in combat, did I have around them folks? What did I know really? And then, somebody bought another round and I lost track of it all until, well, until just now. Hell of a thing…"

Carrie is wiping away a tear when I look up. She says, "You're so much better than you think you are, Dale."

I laugh. I don't have no idea what she's talkin' about, so I just clam up. It is enough that she's happy. She has no idea how happy she makes me by bein' happy. And what in the world do we have to be mad, or…or… suspicious, or just antsy in any way about this morning? This is just the best day. Just the best day ever!

A young guy in a three piece suit walks into the room then. "Mr. and Mrs. Sylvanus? I'm Kevin Kellogg; I'm the new media services leader."

Carrie says, "'Media services'?"

He smiles a boy kinda smile, "I'm the PR guy."

"Oh boy." Carrie says.

He smiles again a little nervous, "Now...now just hear me out."

"Look, Mr....Kevin, we're not idiots. I'm...I'm a nurse. I work at the Hicks Hospice..."

"I...I know...I know about your job. I asked around. And..." He holds up his phone. You know, Google? What not?" He looks kinda proud, the way anybody is if they're doin' good work at their first job.

Carrie hears that and all of a sudden there's fire in her eyes. She don't like the idea that this kid's been snoopin' about our family. What's more, all that's happened has her a little over the edge ya know? Why not. So, anyway, she says, "Yeah? Well...who told you, you could look into our backgrounds?" She calms herself for a second, then says, "With all due respect, sweety, we don't know you. You don't know us. This family has just been through the kind of shock that shakes people up for years. Yes, it all ended well... but...but that's just the point; it hasn't really ended yet. It isn't going to end for a long time. For years! We're just now trying to come to grips with the fact that..." She starts tearing up..."We're grandparents, that our boy is alive and well. That everybody is alive and well. That our boy has a new wife. That Ike has a new wife. That she's from a culture that's, that's different from ours and... and... Look, Dale is an Iraq War veteran and Afghanistan too... you're so young...but try to get your head around that. It hasn't been easy for him for years! For years! What must this be like for him, to save his family, find out that his son has married, well, what up until yesterday he might have seen as the enemy... It's just... You know what that means for heaven's sake? We've had a rough go as a family long before this, but we love each other. We're good people, just trying to sort things out. And now is not the time... Just, just...I don't want to be rude, but no comment."

"But I just..."

And now the fire in her eyes is really blazin'. "No damned comment now or ever!"

He's scared to death now and I don't blame him.

"But just…if we can get out ahead…"

"Son, there's no we involving you and my family. We don't know you. We don't know you at all. I'm trying to be nice here, but you're making it…"

"My bosses…"

I stand up and kinda lean over this kid who is a good six inches shorter and 100 pounds lighter than me.

Now Carrie gets really mad. It's been a hell of a 24 hours and she knows if she don't do something drastic I am gonna toss this kid out of the room. She jumps in front of me and puts her hand on my chest, kinda patting me there.

"I don't give two unholy shits about your fucking bosses! Get out of there! Get out of our faces right now! I tried so hard to be nice to you, but you wouldn't listen… I can only keep my ex-marine husband calm so long, son, before…"

"Can I…"

Carrie can't believe now that he's really gonna go on.

"Take it all and shove it up your ass for all I care, you little bastard!"

I take a step towards him and he runs out of the room. I put my arms around Carrie who is crying. I start to laugh.

"What in the world are you cryin' for? He's the one that oughtta be cryin'. If I was him I'd be cryin'. Probably shittin' myself too."

"I…I hope I did right."

"You kiddin'? You did great! He won't be back buggin' us. And when them other nosey reporters get wind of what…"

"What?"

"When they hear what…"

"Well, well. They're not gonna hear anything, Dale. That's just it. I said 'No comment'."

"Oh, is that how it works?"

"I…yeah…I think so. Oh, dear. I told him to shove it…"

I smile, "Yeah, right up his ass… And ya called him a 'little bastard'. I never heard you say that to anybody, ever. Not even the kids."

"Oh. Oh. He's a kid. I probably really hurt his feelings. He might tell everybody all I said about us just for spite. I better go talk to..."

"No. He wouldn't dare. That boy don't have that kinda sand." I laugh. "Nobody does."

"I, I feel so bad."

"You did just right."

She smiles. "Ya think?"

"Oh hon, I know. First hand."

She swats me in the back of the head, kinda playful like, then smiles and hugs me.

"You're a good man, Dale."

"And you're the best that ever was."

This young nurse walks in then. Kind of looks away but then looks like she's just gotta say something. Carrie looks up first, "What's up...Betsy?"

"Um...Mrs. Sylvanus...um...your...your daughter-in-law wants to talk to your...husband."

"Oh, that's sweet. Thanks, Betsy."

I kinda stand there. Then Carrie says gentle-like, "Dale?"

"Ya...ya... be right there you..."

"I'll watch for when he wakes up." She looks over at Ike. "I'll be there just like when he was little."

I kinda nod, but she doesn't see and I follow the nurse down the hall though I know the way anyway and I start wonderin' what this girl can want. What my daughter-in-law...Donya, can want.

I walk into the hospital room and she's lying back in bed kind of smilin' at somethin' way off and then she looks with those dark eyes and so many memories come flashing and this girl is just, just, what's the word? She's lovely is what. And I just kinda stand there like a little boy. And she reaches down and pats her stomach. She's a tiny girl and her bein' pregnant just makes that even more clear.

"His name will be Jacob," she says in a beautiful accent that just blows me off my feet.

"Jacob," I say without knowing I said it aloud, kinda lookin' at her hand on her belly.

She kind of frowns. "Do you like it, Mr. Sylvanus?"

I stare at her kinda blank for a couple moments and she's lookin' real kinda scared sort of and then I know I better say somethin' right quick, "Oh, ya, ya! It's fine. A fine name: Jacob."

She smiles so wide I think her face might break and she tears up a little. "Oh…I am so pleased."

Then I say somethin' that I don't know where it came from and later Father Bill will say to me with one of his grins, "Oh, you know damned well where it came from!"

"Jacob, son of Isaac."

Now she's smilin' even bigger if that's possible. "Oh yes, yes!" She says, and tries to get up out of bed and I go to her and she takes my right hand and kisses it, and kinda holds it there. And it's so…well not the way folks do things in Hunter. But it's, well, kinda wonderful.

And we just kinda stay that way for a long moment, and I'm not sure I ever want it to end and I think, all of sudden, This girl is my family now. She's like a kind of daughter. I'd walk through fire for her and for her kids. Nothing else matters…Nothing.

Finally she says, "I can never repay."

And then somethin' else comes to me and I surprise myself 'cause maybe I'm changin', I think, in a good way.

"Oh darlin' you just did."

And she reaches out and hugs me and I'm kinda embarrassed, but way more pleased than embarrassed and I kinda hold her there.

"Thank you." I say.

"No, no, thank you. Allah be praised. God is great."

"He is, ain't He?"

And she laughs and laughs and can't stop and just then I can feel Carrie at the door.

She has a real mixed look on her face and she says, "Oh. Oh, Donya I'm so sorry to interrupt. I can come back."

And Donya kind of fixes herself including the look on her

face and says, "Oh no, no. Is my Isaac?"

"Not yet, hon. We'll let you know as soon as he comes back around."

"He is tired I think."

"He is poor thing." Carrie smiles. "And you should be. I gotta borrow this old guy for a second," she says putting a hand on my shoulder.

"Of course, of course."

As soon as we get into the hall I can see there's a problem.

"Jen Hicks is here."

"Oh…lord…did you tell her off too?" I smile.

"No, no, Dale, it's serious. She's trying to help. They're saying horrible things about us."

"Who?"

"Well, the newspapers, TV, the web…it's just awful."

"Well…why? And anyway…what do we care?"

"That's what I said to Jen, but she told me this isn't going to stop unless we make some kind of statement."

"Statement?"

"Yeah, something to 'clear the air' she says."

"Why in the world do they care about two people and a car accident in a little fart of a town in the U.P.?"

"That's what I said."

"And Jen said, what?"

"'The angle?'"

"Huh? She…she said that before. I don't get it."

"Well, come on. I better let her explain it to you. It barely makes any sense to me."

"Well then it ain't gonna make any to me!"

"Just…just c'mon."

When Jen has a go at me, it doesn't make any sense to me. In fact it makes me mad. We're standing there in the hallway and she says 'Angle' about twelve times until I just want to put my fist through a wall.

Carrie puts her hand on my arm and I calm down a little.

Finally, Carrie says, "You mean, this latest thing came

from that..." she looks around "...little shit in the suit from the information office."

Jen eyes me up and says, "I'm afraid so."

"I'll..." I start, but Jen looks at me really hard, a way she never has before. A way only people who know you look at you and I didn't think she knew me that well, but maybe she does.

"You lay a finger on that boy, Dale and you're going to be in jail with your low life friends, and the chatter on the internet is going to get that much worse."

Carrie, says, "Well, what does it say now?"

Jen says, "I don't know, I' haven't looked in a couple of minutes."

I say, "How much can it change in..."

Jen laughs, "You guys really don't get this, do you?"

She holds out her cell phone and shows us a headline from early this morning: 'War Hero and Nurse Wife Save Own Family without Knowing It"

"Oh...so what's..."

Jen puts up a finger and switches to something else: 'Hero Handyman is a Racist, Says Harpy Wife'

"What the hell is a h..."

"There's a lot more: 'Hunky Hero Horrible Dad: Abused Son"

"What the fu..."

"Do you want to see more? There's at least a dozen others and they're coming fast and furious. If you don't get out ahead of it this, this will be the truth."

"What do you mean?" I say. "The truth ain't somethin' you can just make up..."

Jen starts to laugh then covers her mouth. "No Dale, not the real truth. The public truth."

"What's the difference?"

"The real truth is that the two of you are heroes, not because you saved your family, but because you saved people you didn't know. You didn't care what race they were. You didn't even notice it probably. You just tried to help..."

"Like anybody from this town would," Carrie says.

Jen nods, "Yes, but it's a story, see? It's not really life anymore. It's a story now. It's like a myth. Everywhere else people don't give a damn about other people, or at least that's the way the public sees it, so when somebody does, it's a story. It's a big public truth. The trouble is, once you're a public hero like the two of you are now, there's nowhere to go but down. And that's already started because you didn't cooperate with the little twerp from the information office."

"I don't care. Let 'em think what they want. I know what's true!" I say.

"And so does everybody else in Hunter, Dale, but that doesn't matter out there. They're going to hound you and Carrie and Ike and his wife and all the children he has or ever will have until they get what they want: a great story. Then they'll keep milking it until it's dry as a bone."

"So what?" Carrie says. "How long will that take?"

"Weeks at least. And then every time your name comes up for anything else it will come up again and the phone will keep ringing. Sure, it will die down eventually. And you can wait for that, but in the mean time Ike and Donya…is it?" Carrie nods, "And that little girl, your granddaughter, and even the one that isn't born yet, are going to be the playthings of everybody with a camera or a cell phone."

"Christ."

"And that's only the beginning. Have you thought about what's going to happen when Hughie's trial, and the Pups' trial comes up? It's going to come right back to you and you'll be in the spotlight again, asked for comments, 'How could you have hung out with people like that? Do you beat your wife? How long have you been a racist? Is your son a racist too? How does the Native American community feel about a successful, prominent one of their own being married to a racist alcoholic brawler?' And then every time Ike or his wife or his kids or, hell, his grandkids apply for a job or do anything good bad or indifferent here it comes again."

"Okay," Carrie sighs. "What do we do?"

"Leave that to me."

"Jen, no offense…"

"Trust me Carrie. Your family is my family. I promise. I'll get something out there that will straighten this out a bit. I can't make it go away. Nothing can do that, not ever, understand that, but I can make it not quite so bad, so…hysterical, so frantic at least. And I'll take care of that little shit in the information office. He'll wish he was never born."

I smile. "Sure I can't help?"

Jen smiles back, "I won't leave a bruise other than on his boyish ego; you'd break his leg."

She walks away down the hallway, just as Ike and Donya's little girl…Dorri… comes in with an old nurse. Dorri is cute as can be and all cuddled up to the nurse's leg.

"Somebody wants to tell you something, " the nurse says smiling.

"Thank you," this little dark eyed girl says.

Carrie tears up, "Oh sweety, you are so welcome!" She leans down and hugs her. The little girl reaches out and takes Carrie's hand and as they go down the hallway, Carrie is looking at me with tears in her eyes. And I think whatever I've been through, whatever we've been through, whatever we're going to have to go through with even the press or whatever: it's worth it.

I just kind of stand there for a long time in the hall. I don't know how long, and before I know it somebody is talkin'.

"Good day?"

I look up and it's Father Bill. Before I even think of anything I'm hugging him. Now, I don't hug men. I know that makes me bad or what is it, a homo-phobic or whatever they call it, but I don't, so me hugging, even a priest, is a big deal.

"Yeah," I say finally. "Yeah, good day." I pull away from him kind of embarrassed.

Father is half smilin' when I get far enough away to look in his eyes. "I just had to see it. I just had to see you finally getting… and Carrie too, maybe especially Carrie, finally getting all you deserve. You're…you're just the best people I know. Now," he adds real quick like, "now don't let that go to your head."

I have a hard time sayin' anything, but I manage it. "Everybody's been so nice. Well…except for the papers, and the TV…"

"Yeah, I saw some of that. Well…fuck them."

That shocks me quite a bit and I can't help saying, "Father…"

He laughs. "I'll go to confession as soon as possible, but you know, technically that one's not a sin. It's not the Lord's name." He's grinning from ear to ear. "Let's go see your boy, and your granddaughter and this new daughter-in-law."

To say this has been quite a day is, well, not saying enough about it. I keep thinkin' I'm gonna wake up and find myself hung over, back in the storage building out at the lake. The only thing gnawing at me is somethin' father said to me after we did our visitin' with everybody at the hospital and he got me alone again. He says, "Now, Dale, you've made a first step, and you have been aided by Grace in ways that are making my head spin. God is all around you, helping you in everything you do. Well, he always has been, but for some reason he's shouting now instead of just whispering in your ear. I think there are other steps to take and I think you're going to have to keep your head about you to figure out what they are. And along those lines, I have some information for you that I think you really need. It's from Hughie and he said it to me in confidence, not confession, but confidence, and he said he needed me to tell you when I thought the time was right. You've had a Heavenly day, Dale, now I think telling you this is going to bring back the real world…the broken world we live in a little, and that may even be a good thing."

"Well, why don't he just tell me himself? Christ…oops sorry…we had enough time to talk things over all these years. I thought I knew everything about him…"

He kind of looks at me very straight and he says, "Get ready for a shock."

I say, "Oh boy."

"Yeah," he says. "You ready? You should be able to deal

with it, I think, after all that's already happened."

Then he tells me that Hughie told him that he's a homo…I mean he's gay, whatever, you know. What's more, Father tells me that Hughie's always, right from the time we were on the playground in grade school and he saved me, had a thing for me.

After I grab the arm of a chair and hold myself up a minute and stop my own head from spinning, I finally manage to get out, "Is he going to prison, father?"

"Well, he's not going to get the biggest sentence, that'll be Shine if they catch him alive…God knows how that will come out… and I'm no lawyer, but if you beat up a customs officer at his post or participate in such a thing, what with all the paranoia about terrorism, you're setting yourself up to go away for a while."

I'm standing there for a minute and I keep waiting to get all pissed and be ready to kill Hughie myself for bein' a homo and not tellin' me and stuff, but that just doesn't come up. Maybe it's all the other stuff that's happened, maybe I've just growed up. I dunno. Really, half of me wants to be mad at him for bein' that way, like I woulda been even six months ago maybe, but somethin' just stops me. All I can see, somehow, is my old friend there in trouble and what he is don't matter to me at all. And I wonder where that other guy went who used to say all them nasty things about people's races and gays, and all that stuff, and I see Father watching me and he's kinda smilin'.

"What is it, Dale?"

My head is goin' all light. I feel like I'm in somebody else's skin. Finally I get out, "I…I don't know who I am anymore, Father. I ain't mad. I ain't that shocked. I'm thinkin' I mighta knowed this somewheres for a long time. And right now I'm just tryin' to figure how to help my friend."

He starts laughin', then he says. "You're you, Dale. You're a better you I think, the kind of you a guy from Nazareth wanted us all to be." He winks at me. "When all this starts to calm down, maybe you and I will go see your friend?"

"Yeah," I say, lookin' out the windows at all the reporters and the two TV trucks waitin' for Carrie and me or anybody else connected with us to come out. "When's that gonna be?"

Father looks out there too. He laughs. "All will be well. And all manner of things will be well."

"Huh?"

"Lady named Julian of Norwich said that, Dale. She devoted her whole life to Jesus. Some say she was an anchorite, a kind of prisoner for Jesus, walled in, in a church most of her life until she almost died and had some visions. I think maybe we better listen to her and have a little faith."

So we go in to see Ike and he's awake, lying there in bed with a big cast on his leg and a few bandages on his face. I still can't get over all that long hair, even tied back like he keeps it. And then I think, *All that's happened and I'm worried about his damn hair? That's stupid.* And he looks like he's really anxious to see me. And when I come in his arms just go out and I'm hugging him too in a way neither of has ever hugged before or at least not since he was a little boy and all the mess of years when we were going at each other all mad about I can't even remember what…his ideas? His friends? His getting home late? Anyway, all that just goes away, right now. Right this instant. And when we kinda break apart he says, "Oh Dad, I'm so sorry."

I just look at him and I don't really know what to say, but finally I get out, "I don't know for what, Ike. I'm just glad you're okay."

I look over at Carrie and she's crying again holding on to Dorri's hand. And the little girl is looking up at her, like she's just made a good new friend, and she has. And the only things breaking my heart are that I didn't know about the little girl before: my granddaughter. And that I'd made Ike hate me so much that he didn't think he could tell me. Well, that hurts a lot. I gotta do better. And dammit, I will.

"Ike…I….I'm just so glad, too…I…" and that's all I can get out before we hug again.

"Well," Father says, "I've got to get off to Mass. I've got about a fifteen minute margin," he says lookin' at his watch.

Carrie says, "We're coming too." She looks down at Dorri.

The little girl smiles. I look over at Carrie wonderin' if I'm goin' there too. She shakes her head, "No Dorri and me are going to sneak out to Father's car and see if we can't avoid the reporters that Jen's keeping control of. You two old warriors stay here and talk over old times. Donya said it would be fine to see a different church…er…mosque. Didn't your mommy?" Dorri smiles this cute little smile and nods.

So pretty soon they're gone and I still don't know what to say to Ike other than what I've already said, so I just look at him and shake my head.

Finally he says, "What's with all the reporters?"

"I don't get it either, but I guess we're a big story."

"How come?"

"I don't know really. They think your mom and me saved you."

"Well, you did."

"Yeah, but then there's somethin' about me bein' a Marine during Desert Storm, and the family bein' Muslim and how I'm an old…what…racist and I've gotta deal with all these folks comin' into my family."

"Oh," Ike starts laughing a little then a lot. "Isn't that funny?" he says after a minute. "So, so how do you feel about it, Dad?"

"Well…well…to be honest, I'm happier than I've ever been before in my life."

"Really?"

"That's the only thing I'm shocked about, Ike, that I'm somehow a good guy now, not an old drunk that yells at his kid about a bunch of shit…sorry…a bunch of stuff that don't matter a hill of beans."

"Is that what you think you were?"

"Well…yeah."

"Dad, do you have any idea how proud I've always been of you? Do you know how hard it is to live up to what you and Mom have put out there in the world?"

I shake my head. "No…well your mom, sure, but…"

"That's why I left, Dad. Deep down that's why, not all our fights and stuff. I was ashamed and I couldn't stand the way you looked at me when I wasn't measuring up."

My jaw just drops and I look at him and I really am amazed. "Ike…that's…that's just stupid. I'm the one…I'm the one that…"

"Dad, that's not…"

"No, no, listen, if it wasn't for your mom I'd be over in jail with Hughie right now…I'd…"

"Hughie's in jail?"

"Oh…oh…sorry, long story, and too much to take in right now. How's your head?"

"Well, feels like I've been in a bar fight, but I think I'll be okay. The leg is gonna be a pain, though."

"The thing is, Ike. You're okay. That's the thing. That's the only thing. And your kids are all right and your wife. God, she's a pretty thing." He smiles. "You're all right and it's not too late now…that's what worried me, I thought it was too…" I start cryin' and Ike just stares because I never cry and we hug again and I think this is just gettin' silly, but I really don't care and I'm really happy that I don't care. Life is good. Great really.

A couple hours later, Jen finds me in Ike's room. Donya's in there by then. She's sittin' over in a corner lookin' around at all of us. She just kinda owns a room, ya know? I don't know how to put it. You can't look away from Donya. Awful pretty. I see why Ike picked her out. Not just her looks but…her way. Anyway, Jen Hicks gots a way too.

"The press people want a statement."

"Oh jeez, Jen, can't you…" I say.

"I've already given them six and they're not interested in me anymore. They want to hear from you."

"I wouldn't even know what to say."

"Just say what you think. That this is all great and that you love your new family, and that this is the best day of your life."

"Well…that is what I think."

"Then say that."

I take a big breath and blow it out.

Ike starts laughing. "My Dad the celebrity."

I look at him with a little grin, "Maybe you'd like to make a statement?"

"He may have to later, but right now it's your turn." Jen says.

"Okay." I say and smile at everybody, then go out.

Jen squeezes my arm, "You're gonna do great."

"I've never been so scared in my life."

"That's why you'll do great, because you're really scared. You're really you. No politician can fake what you are, Dale: a genuine hero."

"Oh, now that's just buillshit!"

"And the fact that you think it is just proves it more." She grins at me.

When we get out there in the parking lot, it's just crazy. It's about 5:30, still plenty of light, but the camera lights are just blinding and there's just a crazy bunch of people. I almost wet myself, I swear just walkin' up to the microphones.

"Um…" I say, "…hello."

Somebody from behind the lights, a woman, that's all I can tell and only from the voice, says, "Do you consider yourself a hero?"

"No. No, not really at all."

"But you saved three people…four really."

"Well, they were family."

"You didn't know that though, at the time, right?" A guy with a deep voice says.

"No. No I didn't."

"Would it make any difference if they weren't?" A different woman.

"No, I don't suppose. But you know, Carrie, my wife was the real hero. She did most of the medical work. I just…got them out of the cars, did a little mouth to mouth."

"Were you ever afraid for yourself?" Another guy.

"Wasn't much time to think like that."

"So, no, then." The first woman again. All them reporters

laugh.

"No, no, I guess I wasn't afraid. Like I say, no time."

"Do you see any irony in the fact that you saved Muslims and not so long ago you were shooting at them." The deep voice.

"Well…well… Irony. Wasn't never very good at English." They laugh again, and it's kinda like the way the lake summer people laugh. Well, Pop told me how to handle that. I start to feel more kinda at ease. "… but if I take your meaning, you know, it was a good while ago, but I don't know if I ever thought about anybody's religion in either case. They was just people."

"So then, you're not a racist?" Another woman.

"Well…I can't say I didn't used to be. I guess I probably said some words I shouldn't of enough times…and I know I thought some things…"

"But you don't say or think them anymore?" Deep voice.

"No. I guess I can say that. I couldn't a said that maybe even a week ago, though, maybe. I ain't nobody's saint."

"What changed?" First woman.

"Well, my boy was comin' home and I'd just been out on a bender with…with my friend and I felt just awful and I talked to Father Bill and then Carrie and all of a sudden it didn't seem like such a good idea to be a loud mouthed drunk anymore."

There's a couple chuckles at that and they kinda end quick.

"Is that how you would describe yourself…until… recently?" Another fella.

"Yes. Yes I guess so."

"What do you think of all the attention?" Same guy.

"Well…well to be honest I don't know what to make of it. Carrie and me, really, would just like to get back to our lives."

"What do you think of Mr. and Mrs Abbasi coming to meet you and your wife." First woman.

"What?" I look over at Jen. She shrugs, her eyes kinda big. "I…I didn't know they was comin'!"

The reporters all laugh. "Well, are they welcome?" Deep voice.

"Oh yeah. Yeah. Hell…I mean yeah. They're welcome

any time. We're…we're honored if they're comin'. When are they comin'?"

The reporters laugh even harder.

"The word is some time tomorrow." One of the women.

"The 'word' from who? Well…well we'll have to cook up somethin' special."

"Do you stand behind your friends?" First guy who spoke.

"Which friends are those?"

"The…what is it? 'The Pups'?" Same guy.

"Oh, well them guys been my friends my whole life, so yeah."

"Do you know where…Shine is?" Still the same guy.

"No, but I hope he turns himself in." I kinda look at the lights and say, "Shine, if you're seein' this, turn yourself in!"

There's kinda some little laughs that stop before they get started.

"How come you weren't with them when they got in trouble?" Deep voice.

"Well…well… that's the thing. If I hadn't had my…my awakening you might say, if my boy hadn't been comin' and if it weren't for Carrie and Father and Big Ol'…Rex…well I woulda been and I'd be behind bars with them now, too."

"So how come you haven't been to visit them?" First guy.

"Well…I guess, I've kinda been advised not to. Besides, we're pretty busy here right now."

"Advised by your wife?"

"Yeah, and like I say, Father and Big Ol'."

"So are you going to visit them?" First woman.

"Yeah, I guess I will when this all settles out."

"Mr. Laurila,.." Deep voice.

"Who?"

"Hugh Laurila…" Same.

"Oh. Oh Hughie, yeah?'

There's a little bit of laughter. "Hughie says he saved your life when you were kids."

"Well, yeah, maybe, she was a pretty big girl."

There's big laughs. I kinda warm up and Jen looks uneasy. "Yeah, she beat me up pretty bad, so maybe he did save me, yeah."

"He says you owe him one." Deep voice.

"Well, there's a lotta back and forth there. Lotta water under the bridge."

"Do you plan to help him?" First woman.

"I do. I think I can say I do. Just as soon as I can."

"Is there any truth to the story that you and Hughie are or were lovers." First guy.

Jen's head kinda jerks up. She steps up to the microphone, "That's enough questions for now. Let's let this man get back to his..."

I look over and kinda shake my head telling her it's all right. She stares at me hard, but I nod. "Well, I just found out about that."

"It was news to you that Mr. Laurila is gay?" Deep voice.

"Yeah, yeah it is, though I guess somewhere in the back of my brain I always kinda felt maybe he was. Didn't really know I knew that until today if you follow me..."

"So it was an unrequited love?" Deep voice.

I look over at Jen. She rolls her eyes then sighs then kinda nods. "Yeah, yeah, I'm bein' told that's true."

Again big laughs.

"Well did you know he loved you or not?" Second woman.

"I think so. Yeah, I guess I did."

"Do you love him?" Deep voice. And it seems like he's gettin' excited for some reason.

"Well...yeah...I guess you could say, but not in that way."

"What way?" Deep voice.

"Well...I ain't a gay man."

"Are you sure?" Some nervous laughter.

"Well, I got three kids and a grandkid and another on the way, and a gorgeous wife, so I guess I'm pretty sure."

Huge laughs.

Jen steps in again. "Mr. Sylvanus is done for now. Just shoot any further questions my way. Let's let him go talk to his family and maybe get some sleep."

Somebody shouts as we're walkin' away, "Have you ever had any gay experience with Mr. Laurila or any other man?"

"No." I say. Then I add, "I think I'd remember."

"Let's go." Jen says.

"How'd I do?"

"I've seen worse."

"I give 'em too much to write about?"

"Well…the gay stuff. Where did that come from?"

"Father just told me today. How did them reporters know?"

She sighs again. "They find out everything. My guess is they got it out of Chessy. Somebody was fishing for information and those guys bit like prize trout. Has Hughie kept this secret up to now?"

"Yeah. I guess so. I didn't know until today."

"That's not good. How do you think he'll react when he finds out everybody knows he's gay."

"Huh. I don't know. He ain't real stable. Now I think about it, it could get pretty bad. I wonder…maybe I better talk to Father."

"I'll call him. Maybe he can head this off before it gets too bad."

"Oh. Yeah. I'd hate that." We walk a couple steps and I kinda, real gentle, take her arm and stop her. "Jen, why is my life so good all sudden like and their lives are the worst they've been? Hughie and Chessy in jail and Shine, maybe about to get himself killed. One have anything to do with the other, you figure?"

"Well…maybe Dale, but you sure aren't to blame."

"How come?"

"You grabbed a hold of your life and pulled yourself up. What they did was their choice. The only difference there would have been if you'd been there, is you might have ended up in jail with them, or you might have sacrificed yourself and wound up in there alone. Best and worst case scenario? You somehow manage to keep them out of jail, at the same time Ike has his car crash and you're not there to save your family. Want to push this line of reasoning any further?"

I take a breath. "Hell, no."

She nods. "Let's leave it alone, then. You're doin' great, Dale. Don't blame yourself for whatever happens from here on out. Let's just look out for this family of yours. Let's have you get to know them at least."

"Yeah, yeah, you're right. I don't hardly know them."

"Want some coffee?"

"Sure."

"I'll meet you in Ike's room."

By the time Jen shows up with the coffee, Carrie has already shown back up from church, and the first thing she says is, "Dale… honey…what in the world did you tell them about yourself? Wasn't Jen…"

Right then Jen walks in. "Jen, what the f…?"

"I know I know. I didn't see it coming because I didn't know. We may need to get somebody else to….handle the media. This is getting out of hand."

"No, no," I say. "It's you or nobody."

"Right." Carrie says.

Jen kinda sighs. "Okay. Okay. I let you down. I'm sorry." She looks around, then says, "But I didn't know Hughie was gay."

"They asked me if my husband was 'gay curious', the reporters who were waiting for us outside church."

"Oh my God!" Jen looks at her cell phone and clicks a few buttons. She kinda laughs for a second…then looks concerned and looks at us. "Well, you might as well know the worst." She holds up the phone to us and there's a headline from one of them, sites, that says, "Racist Closeted Former Marine Had 'Awakening'"

"What the fuck?!" I scream and Ike wakes up.

"Dad?"

"Oh, oh, sorry, Ike. So sorry. It's nothing. Go back to sleep."

"What can we do, Jen?" Carrie says, all serious.

"I think we're going to have to call one of the big new outlets–a network. You guys go on as a family, make a statement and see if we can't make this as truly wholesome as it is and shut this damned thing down."

I nearly wet myself again. "Oh no…"

Carrie looks at me and says, "How long you wanna be 'Racist Closeted Former Marine?"

I take a big breath. "Okay."

Thursday, 7:36 a.m.

I didn't sleep. Not a wink. How could I? We're gonna be on the national morning show. Well, really we're kinda on there now. They've got us all together. Carrie and Me, Kelly and Donny, Ike and Donya, and Dorri. We're here in Ike's hospital room and there's cameras everywhere and lights even brighter than the ones for that shit storm news conference out in the parking lot. Jen is here too. She set it up. She figures if we tell our story right out to… America…well, maybe all these press people will leave us alone.

"Not right away probably, but soon. That's what I hope anyway."

Don't seem real, none of it. Anyway, we're here on 'standby' waiting for them to talk in our ears. Ike is in the bed, and we're all around him. Carrie and the kids and me on one side and Dorri and Donya on the other. And Jen's here, too, like I said, as our… what…spokeswoman. It's funny, Jen was really worried that Donya wouldn't understand, but I think she understands it better than anybody. She said to me, "Mr. Sylvanus…" I tried to get her to call me Dale, but she just smiled that wonderful smile and dropped her eyes. "Mr. Sylvanus, if you are Muslim in America right now, and anything happens to bring attention to you, you are better to speak up and tell them what you think than to let them assume the worst. Believe me, I understand."

She don't look too happy about it right now, though, and neither do any of us except for Donny who thinks it's great. We all got these terrible smiles on our faces and well…here goes. They do some kind of introduction for it, and I can hear the morning guy with the dark hair and big blue eyes and what's it…Mary Lee, you know the pretty one with the big teeth from the network,… talkin' and then all of a sudden…

"Mr. Sylvanus, so nice of you…so nice of you all to let us in on this family situation."

"Well…" I say, when air comes back into my lungs. "Don't seem like we had much choice…"

I hear some laughter from wherever the news people are,

New York...whatever...then Jen shoots me a look and says, "Jim, the press was all over the story anyway, and the family just thought they'd better tell it themselves..."

"Yes," Jim says, "there have been some wild stories around, but our network wasn't part of that. Mrs. Sylvanus could you tell us what happened?"

Carrie almost jumps out of her skin, but then does a real good job, in that calm nurse voice telling everything that happened.

Mary Lee says, "Are you proud of your husband?"

Carrie looks over at me, "You bet. I've never been prouder, not even when he was serving his country. He did great."

"Ah..." I start but then all of a sudden Donny is talkin'...

"And we really like our new relatives! They're all...well, they're cute and brown."

Ike, who's a little under the drugs they got him on right now starts laughin' and Donya looks away from the camera laughin' real hard. Jen looks like she's gonna faint. We can hear them all laughin' through the ear plugs. Finally, Jim says, "What's next for the Sylvanus family?"

Jen pipes up, "Well Jim, later today the Abbasies will be joining the family for dinner at an undisclosed location and then everybody in Hunter is just hoping we can get this family back to some semblance of a normal life."

Mary Lee says, "We understand there might be a book deal."

I shoot a look at Jen. She gives me her calm eyes, but I can see she's a little nervous around the edges

"Well, there have been offers, but we are very far from moving on, in that direction."

And then, quick as lightning, it's over. And all the lights go away and we're alone as a family again and we're all breathing.

Carrie lets out a big breath then she and Jen hug each other and start laughin' hysterical like. I will never understand women.

Donny is just grinnin' from ear to ear and Kelly swats him. "What?"

"Just had to open your mouth didn't you?"

Carrie says, "Now Kelly your brother did fine."

Donya laughs and says, "He did very well indeed."

"Funniest thing I ever heard." Ike says.

So. So here we are. This is my new family. I'm tryin' to let that sink in.

"What's this about a book deal?" Carrie says.

"Well," Jen says, " I didn't want to bother you with it today. There have been offers. It's lots of money."

"Really?" Carrie says.

"A book," I say. "What in the world about?"

Jen says, "Um...you."

"Me? What would there be to...no way."

Carrie isn't so sure. And I'm thinkin' it ain't like her to be so interested in money, but I can't hardly blame her. All my shenanigans over the years ain't made us over rich. "How much money, Jen?"

Jen whispers in her ear.

"Holy..."

"Yes. It's a lot. That's just one offer. We could probably get more if we play one against the other."

Carrie says, "Well, the only authors we'll accept are you... or maybe your brother Ben or...or both of you."

"Oh, they'd never go for that; they'll want their own authors, I'm sure."

I say. "Well, tell them vultures no way!"

Carrie says, "Let me talk with you later."

"No way. I ain't done nothin' in my life worth writin' about. Nothin' good anyway."

"We'll get back to you," Carrie says, then looks over at Donya, "So, we're so looking forward to meeting your folks."

"Oh, they will be very honored."

"I can't imagine what they're making of all this."

Donya smiles, "It is an unusual situation, but it will be well."

"Yes," I say. I think about what Father said about that anchor lady, who talked about all bein' well. It's kinda the same. I'm really startin' to like this girl, my daughter-in-law. I really hope she's right and Father's right. I think they are. "Yes it will." I say.

So, Carrie takes Jen and me out into the hall and we leave the kids to talk over things, make plans and stuff for the rest of the family that's comin',what not. And Carrie looks at me and says, "Listen to what Jen has to say."

And then Jen tells me there's a couple different book places want the story, and a movie guy too I guess, and they're offering like $300,000 as a whatchacall…advance. And then more for the sales. And I just stand there with my jaw hangin' down.

"Wait…$300,000?! And that's before we even write a word?"

Jen says,"Well…you don't ever write a word, Dale. You just talk to'em and they write it down."

"That's the part I don't like." Carrie says. "How do we know what they're going to write?"

"Well, you sort of don't. And from what they've said to me so far, you wouldn't really have final approval of what went in the book. They'd just be buying the rights to run it once they interview you. Now, if you don't like what they come out with, you could sue them…"

Carrie says, "Well, that's why we want you to write it. Or Dr. O'Brian, if you don't want to…"

"Well, this wouldn't really be in Ben's line. He did work for the Hunter Tales for a little bit, right out of high school, but he's more of a poet. Though he could do it. I could talk him into it. I don't think he'd want to though. I've done more of this kind of writing…"

I say, "So why don't you do it? Don't ya wanna?"

"Well, yes! Sure! I absolutely want to, but I'm not sure the publisher would want somebody so untested, and somebody who's in your camp."

"What the…what's a 'camp'…we ain't got a camp other than…"

Jen laughs. "No, I mean on your side."

"Oh."

"Well," Carrie says, "how much less if it's you that's writing it?"

"Well, we could publish ourselves, see what we make, but that won't be near as much, not even close really. I might be able to work something with one of the publishers for a lot less advance. I could interview you guys, or you could write down your ideas and I could work from that. But this is going to go away soon. This other book offer, I mean. I give it about a week before the publicity dies down and interest with it. Maybe less."

Carrie says, "Well, have you talked to your brother?"

"Which one? Ben's with Val somewhere up in Canada near Flin Flon. They're off the grid, can't be reached. I know that for sure because I haven't heard from Ben, and if he heard about how you're being treated, Dale, he'd be on the phone screaming or on his way back here ready to clock some reporter.

I laugh, "Ya, I know. I've seen him that way."

"My other brother, Jake…"

"Ya, I know Jake too. I guided with him once when he come up with some mucky muck."

"Well, he's a big deal lawyer you probably know, and he's already called and told me he's at your service, can be here on a plane inside a day if we want him. And I talked to him about the book people too and he's willing to help with that. He knows people in government, too, lots of 'em. So, anyway, whatever we need that way."

Carrie is thinkin' and looks at me. "What do you think?"

"Well, I don't like it, but it's hard to pass up that kind of money. That's seven, eight years of what we make easy…"

"And that's just the advance." Jen says.

"Well…" I say, "maybe talk to Father?"

"That's a good idea." Carrie says. "But he's kinda busy with Hughie right now."

"Uh oh…" I say. "This somethin' new?"

"Well, he's over there with him now, Hughie's pretty upset about what's in the press."

"You mean, what I said?"

"I'm afraid so. He's blaming Father for telling you, and then he's blaming you for talking about it."

"Oh...jeez...But he told father to tell me! It's not Father's..."

Jen says, "You got ambushed, Dale. Happens all the time and to folks that work with the media a lot more than you do."

"I didn't mean to cause him trouble..."

Carrie says, "After all the trouble Hughie has caused you? Caused us? I wouldn't worry about it!"

Jen says, "Right! This isn't your fault at all. But maybe you could go over to the jail in the Soo before your dinner today?"

"Oh, what about Ike and..."

Carrie says, "They'll all still be here and we've gotta get Jen and Doc's camp all set for the dinner anyway...not much you could do. You head on over there, help Father, and we'll be all set for the dinner by the time you get back."

"Ya...ya. Okay. But, Jen, I want you to write the book. That's a lock. We gotta take less money that's fine, but I don't trust them vultures..."

"Well, I'll see what I can do to make that work."

"I think that's good thinking, Dale." Carrie says. "When did you get so smart?"

"I didn't." I say. "I just listen to smart women."

They both laugh.

"Okay, team," Carrie says, still kinda laughin'. "Let's make this work!"

★★★

So, things ain't great at the jail. Hughie is about half outta his mind and Father's doin' a lotta sighin' and shakin' his head.

"Nobody sold you out, Hughie!" I say, but he ain't listenin'.

"Ya, great, big shot! You get to be the big hero I get to be the queer goin' to jail to get my ass reamed!"

"Hughie," Father says. "Calm down." He gets him some water from the cooler in the cell hall and walks it over to him. "Now just drink this and then let's say some Our Fathers and see what develops."

Hughie drinks the water then tosses the paper cup out into the hall. "Fuck you and your fuckin' prayers, Father. You ain't in here."

"No I'm not, Hughie. And it isn't me who beat up a customs officer either. And it wasn't Dale either so…"

"He shoulda been there!"

"Why? So he could be in there with you? For somebody who claims to love Dale, you sure sound like you'd like to drag him down with you."

Hughie almost cries. "He should be in here with me!"

"And if he was his kids and grandkids would be dead! Are you that selfish, Hughie?"

Father just holds a pretty powerful look at Hughie, and for a second Hughie tries to be all tough, but then he breaks.

"No. No." He takes a breath. "I guess not. I'm just worked up."

"Okay. Let's work you down then. Our Father, who art in heaven…"

It was amazin' what prayin' did for all of us. Made us kinda focus…don't know how to put it…but when we was done prayin' on that great big old rosary of Father's…I used to fall asleep in church doin' all them prayers when I was a kid…anyway, when we was done, we was all calm. Hughie even smiled. By the time we left that jail I felt good about it. Oh, I know'd Hughie would give me more trouble and probably try to get his own book out too, more power to him. I don't care what he says, but at least for now he was calm.

When we get outside them damned reporters are waitin' for us again, about five of 'em with microphones, one with just a notepad. One TV truck. Father has a great way of handlin' it. He bows his head, so I bow my head and he starts in, "Oh Lord, give us this moment of peace to pray for our friends and neighbors and for these men and women telling the stories which need to be told." And he goes all quiet for quite a while, and I see some of the reporters got their heads dropped too and all of a sudden I feel father grab my shirt sleeve and start walkin', takin' me with him.

And before I know it, and with them reporters still yellin', we're all of a sudden in Father's car and on our way with the TV lights 50 feet away and doin' us no harm.

I laugh and look over at Father as we pull away. "That was pretty slick, Father."

He grins, "Old priest's trick: distract'em with prayer and use the Catholic guilt to keep'em quiet. Must have been some old Catholic school kids in that little bunch of reporters."

I laugh. "It seemed to work with Hughie too."

Father looks out at the road and gets serious. "Prayer's no joke, Dale." He grins. "At least not always. I'll admit sometimes it's mumbo jumbo, abracadabra...did you know that "abracadabra actually means, 'In the name of the Father, and of the Son, and of the Holy Ghost?' Well, it does, and some priests and officials of all faith's use prayer in the worst ways, like it's some magician's trick; but prayer is real, Dale, it works at the very least, to focus people, to calm them down. Science has even shown it, though that's not always the best measure. It gives people peace. But there's more, too, a real conversation with the infinite that happens if you practice prayer often enough. And sometimes, through Grace, even if you're not a regular practitioner."

"Do you think God really answers?"

"He ALWAYS answers, Dale, but sometimes the answer is no. And sometimes the answer is "Wait" when you think you need a yes, right now, more than ever before. It's only later when you develop some discernment, and that can only happen through a lot of prayer and meditation, or to certain special people with the right sensibilities, that in a particular case, you come to understand that the answer had to be no. It's hard though, because, like I said, the no's often come in our darkest hour and we don't see any light in them and we despair. But it's like Julian of Norwich talks about in her little parable about the servant, you just have to look in the right direction and then you'll see God is watching. Look away from your own troubles and you'll see he's paying attention, giving you what you need. It's hard to know that, though, because, just like Julian, we're all too human."

I think that over for a minute. "Well Father, I don't understand most of that…"

He laughs. "That's okay, Dale. You will. And I don't understand all of it myself, only some of it some of the time. I'm pretty human too."

So we start talkin' about this book deal and Father Bill does what he always does: he asks me what I think. And of course that's not what I want, but what he was just sayin' kinda clicks in, cause maybe talkin' about it is what I need. And I tell him it's so much money that I don't think we can pass it up. That it could do an awful lot of good for my family and for Ike and his family, and maybe even for the church.

Father laughs, "Well, leave the church out of it. We're rich enough and you do enough, you and Carrie and your mom and dad, for our little church at the lake."

"Well, we could make some improvements out there, fix some things up."

"Okay, Dale. I'll make you a deal: if you take the bulk of it for you and yours the church will take a little donation maybe to shore up the steeple and buy a few icons. But first, you need to decide if you really want this book. And what the cost will be."

"No, it's all free, Father. We just have to get interviewed and we're hopin' maybe we can get Jen to be the writer."

He laughs. "Oh that Jen is a bird! She's always got ideas. She's always telling me what the Church should be doing. And you don't know how many talks I've had with her brother Ben, where her name comes up. She just drives him crazy."

I laugh. "Yeah, Doc talks to me about her a lot too. Seems like they really kinda love each other, but they drive each other nuts. Lotsa brothers and sisters are like that, I guess."

"That's about the size of it. Families are like that. Wish I could get them both to come to Mass more. They're both really good Catholics; they just don't know it. They're just Vatican II liberal Catholics, like most of us were in the 60's and 70's. And old liberals die hard."

"I don't understand that, either, Father."

"That's okay, Dale. Now as to that money, take it or don't. Do what your heart tells you. I can't make that call for you. You're right, it could do a lot of good, but how are you going to feel about telling them your story, especially if it's not Jen."

"Well, if it ain't Jen, or Doc, I ain't tellin' them my story."

"I think that's good thinking, Dale. I think that makes sense."

"Thanks, Father. Now what in the world am I gonna do about Hughie?"

Father doesn't even look up from the road. "Hughie is up to Hughie. Hughie is gay, Dale. And that's a hard thing to face for him, growing up the way you guys did. He can't help how he feels about you or about being attracted to men. It's a way people are born. And he's going to have to learn that there's nothing wrong with being who he truly is. No matter what some people you guys grew up with might say. No matter what some people in my Church say for that matter. Anyway, he's going to have to come to grips with that himself. And it's not going to be easy to do while he's in prison, which might be for a while, unless some lawyer finds him a way out."

"What about Chessy? And…Shine? Shine and me never got along very well…but I hope he don't get killed."

"Those fellas hardly know they're alive, Dale. The two of them don't share a complete brain between them." He looks over at me to see if I'm surprised he said that, and I am, but I manage to nod. "I know that sounds pretty mean for a priest, but we're talking truth here. I don't want to mess around. I don't know…I don't see them seeing the light of day for a long time. And it's not your fault; so wipe that look off your face." Father looks a little irritated. "Dale, sometimes I think you're too good a Catholic. Nobody should be carrying as much guilt around as you do. Let Jen write this book about you. That's my final word. And I'll try to help you keep the reporters away for the next couple days. You know they're going to be all over that dinner today. And if they catch Shine…or God forbid…he gets himself shot, they'll be after your reaction."

"Ya. I just hope Teddy Grace gets to Shine first. Teddy's

got a way of handlin' people. Once I come up on Teddy standin'
outside the River House and there was a couple of Chessy's cousins
goin' at each other and Teddy was just standin' there. I was sober at
the time, and I walked up and asked him what he was doing and
why he wasn't stopping' it. Teddy says, 'Well Dale, what's the point
of my getting into the middle of that? Let them wear themselves
out. Then I'll take'em both in.'"

   Father kind of laughs at that. Finally he says, "Trooper
Grace sounds like the man for the job."

   "Ya, If anybody can bring Shine in without shootin' him,
Teddy can. And about that dinner, I don't think them reporters
will be there; we're havin' it out to Doc's place. They don't even
know…"

   "They'll find out. What's more they're going to bring Ben's
name into it, make him seem like a more famous writer than he is.
That gives them one more tie in for their story, wraps it up with
a neat little bow." Father laughs for a second. "That's going to piss
Ben off to no end. Good thing he's not here."

   "Do you think we should have it somewhere else?"

   "It isn't going to matter where you have it. It's going to be
a circus."

   "That's…that's too bad. Donya's family sounded very nice
over the phone. I just wanted to meet them kinda quiet like. And,
well, I'm a little nervous about it. Only time I was ever around Arab
people, I was in a uniform. I was shootin' at'em. They know that.
The um…Abbasies…Donya's people, they're real educated. He's a
history professor, I guess, and she's some kinda doctor."

   "OBGYN, baby doctor. And from what I hear, a renowned
one."

   "Famous?"

   "Yup," wrote some books of her own, according to Jen.

   "So…how are we gonna get around them reporters?"

   "I don't know, Dale. Maybe do the same thing we just did
there. Maybe pray? Or maybe just learn to develop a tolerance for
praise…and abuse." He grins at me.

   I didn't have no idea what he meant by that, but I laughed

'cause I could see he was joshin' me. I seem to like Father Bill more and more.

We take a back way out to Doc's, but it don't matter. It's just like Father said. They are all over that place, them reporters. A couple of the same ones who were at the jail are there, and one more TV truck. There's about ten of them, this time. As soon as we get out of the car one yells out, "Isn't this the home of the famous poet, Ben O'Brian?"

I look up and Jen is holding the back door open. Father stops and does his distract'em prayer thing again and I rush on into the house. I hear one of the reporters yell to Father, "Are Hughie and Dale lovers?"

Father says, "We should all love each other, my son…" and he steps through the doorway real quick like and closes the door behind him."

"Hello, Jen."

"That was pretty slick. Maybe I should dress as a nun when I'm representing the family."

"Oh now, that would be sacrilegious. I couldn't sanction that." and he winks at her.

"The Abassies are about a half hour away. How do we get them in here with the least fuss?" Jen says.

Father says, "Ecumenical summit."

Jen says, "Huh?"

"Leave it to me."

When the Abassies' car pulls up outside, Father still ain't at no loss. He goes out there like he's some kinda mayor or somethin' and says, "As salaam alaikum!" That means, "peace be with you" father told me before, and said I should say it to the Abassies. Funny, I'd heard it in Iraq and Afghanistan, but never stopped to wonder what it meant. Just looked at it all as nonsense words I guess. Kinda funny, we say the same thing at Mass. Don't know, but I was thinkin' about it later and maybe people really ain't so different. Maybe all these wars ain't about much of anything. Anyway, the Abassies look real mixed up for a second when Father says that, but then both smile real wide, and say, "Alaikum salaam!"

And Father rushes them into the camp before the reporters can fire more than a few questions. Now, none of them vultures go away for another hour or so, and they filmed the whole thing, but at least it's over with.

Dr. Abassi, who is this tall, dark, nice lookin' fella, looks at Father and says, "That was very shrewd, good Father!"

Father grins from ear to ear. Just 'Bill', thanks." He puts out his hand. "It's so very nice to meet you Mr. and Mrs. Abassi.

"Oh please, Dalir and Farrin."

"And these are your...in-laws! Dale and Carrie and their son Donny and their lovely daughter Kelly."

We all shake hands. I remember to say "Salaam alaikum" and the Abassis are pleased and surprised again, I think. I can't even think about what Ike probably told them about me. But, maybe, it was all good. I been so wrong about what he thought to begin with. But then there's all this "Gay racist" stuff in the papers.

Carrie says, "So sorry about all the reporters."

"Not at all," Mrs. Abassi, who I can see Donya is the spittin' image of, says, "Not at all. It is the world, not you who caused this. Thank you so much for all you've done for our daughter and the children. We do love Ike so."

Dr. Abassi says, "He is a good man."

"Well, thank you." I say, "we're just real happy to get to know 'em again ourselves. And we're...proud...to know all of you. We just....well, a lot has happened."

"Yes," Mrs. Abassi says. "I hope we will get to talk about it all."

After the dinner that Donya planned out for us with Carrie, we sit and talk for a while about a lot of things. Father and Mr. and Mrs. Abassi and Donya seem to understand each other in a way I never get, unless Father explains it to me. But it's good just to hear the smart, friendly, jokey talk. Father leaves for some hospital visits after a while, deals with them reporters slick as snot. They're down to just a guy with a notepad and one TV reporter now, when he goes back to his car. I dunno. I don't really get how he does that, just talks his way around people with a smile and a priest's collar, and everybody comes out smiling.

It's funny, when we get done talking with our new family that night, I really don't feel like the same person anymore. It's weird. I don't hardly feel like I know that guy I used to be only a couple days ago. I don't understand it, not even close, but I think a lot of folks, like the Abassies, understand it better than me. 'Course, that ain't surprisin' 'cause all of 'em are smarter than me. Sometimes I think I'm the dumbest one in the family and it's them that's makin' me smarter. Carrie gets mad at me when I say stuff like that, and I can't say I really understand that, either, but it makes me feel better. I guess as Ma used to say when I didn't do so good in school, "You're plenty smart enough for me, Dale. What's better, you're good."

I never believed that last part neither, but Carrie says that's one 'a my big problems, "Everybody knows you're good but you, and you keep tryin' to prove you're not."

She said that once, calm as can be, when I was drunk and actin' like a damned fool. It was just before she shut the door in my face the first time.

There's an awful lot here. There's an awful lot just this week that I'm gonna be years sortin' out. What's more, you'd think the old nightmares would be comin' back about the road in Afghanistan and some of the things from Iraq, but no. Not at all. 'Course I ain't slept much, but when I'm tired, I sleep good, and I'm awful tired now.

We ask the Abassies to stay right here with us at Doc's camp in the bunks. They seem a little unsure, but are more than nice about it. It's funny. They're so polite. It's like if it's what we want, it's what they want. I gotta introduce them to Ma and Pop. They're gonna love 'em. Them good manners…well, they're my folks' kinda people. With all that stuff you see on the news and all… and all them politicians yellin' about Muslims and terrorists…well.. Who'd a thunk that?

The Abassies put so much stock in Carrie and me savin' everybody. Just like everybody else done, in a way, but so much nicer than them damned reporters. 'Course, I guess them reporters are just doin' their jobs too.

Well, as I'm goin' to bed, I peek out the window and I see there's still one reporter out there, the TV guy with his crew, smokin' cigarettes, drinkin' coffee. Still doin' their jobs.

And most everybody from my family, all but Ma and Pop and Ike, is safe inside, just goin' on with life.

Friday, 6:00 a.m.

I have a dream about Afghanistan, but a nice one. A sunrise out on the desert, in the mountains. Beautiful in a way I forgot about. Like over Lake Superior, wide like, but dry and cold. Hadn't thought about that in a long, long, time. And then the smell of cookin', like I smelled lots of times goin' through little towns and neighborhoods in the cities over there. I wake up and I realize the Abbasies are cookin'. I stumble up outta that low bunk in the small bedroom and walk out to see the Abbasi ladies, and the little girl, my granddaugter Dorri, and Carrie, Kelly and Mr. Abbasi and even Donny all cookin'.

"Good morning! Good morning! Mr. Sylvanus!" Dr. Abassi says.

"Oh…oh…I'm just Dale, I told ya." I smile at him. Can't seem to help it.

He smiles and it warms ya right through. He's like… what?…so kinda right here, right now. He ain't tryin' to figure out what's comin' next. He's just livin' his life. Lot of educated folks ain't like that. They're always tryin' to show ya, somethin' else, how smart they are, what not. Not the good ones, though. He, Mr. Abassi, Dr. I mean, he's got that good teacher thing goin' kinda like Doc O'Brian, only younger and a lot darker. He's there with ya, and he's tryin' to teach ya somethin', but it ain't to show ya how smart he is; it's because he cares about ya, ya know?

"Well," he says smilin' a little mischiefy like smile, "'just Dale', I am just Dalir," and he comes over and hugs me, which I ain't used to, but I'll have to be. "And I hope, that since now we are brothers forever, you will always call me that." And he's got that accent that kinda talks to ya about that whole countryside in the war zones and outside 'em and he's got them dark eyes, like all them people that used to crowd around us, used to scare us guys in uniform really, 'cause we never knowed which one was gonna have a bomb strapped to him. I look at this fella and his wife, and, well, my granddaughter, and hell, they're my in-laws and I know that none of them wouldn't never do nothin' like that and for the first time ever, I think, I know! that people are just people and some are…well…crazy as batshit…and some are really good, really good like the Abassies. And then I think about Carrie bein' Indian herself, er 'Native American' or 'First People' or whatever, growin' up on the rez, and dealin' with all kinda Indians and government folks who come out there: some real assholes and some not. She's been tryin' to explain this all to me for years, but until right then, right that second, I didn't really get it at all, not even close. And I think, "Damn. How could I not get it? It's easy as pie."

And I look over and Carrie and Mrs….Farrin…are holdin' hands and cryin' watchin' me and…Dalir…hug. Well, it's a real good couple seconds there. I think I'll remember it for a long time.

Well, it's hard to top that in a day or a whole life I guess, and we sure don't top it that day, because the day gets worse for a lotta reasons. I'll tell ya true, the day kinda went to shit, but not because of anything my new Afghani family done. It started again with them reporters outside and they all played a part in what come after, but that wasn't it neither. There was a bunch of other stuff that happened. Where should I start?

Maybe with the dog runnin' away. What with all the commotion, we thought our dog didn't need to be out at O'Brian's camp so we brung Lester over to Ma and Pop's. But a course, he wasn't havin' it. He was gonna go find his family even though he's been over to that house on and off most days most of his life. Them dogs know stuff, I seen it huntin' with'em. I dunno…well, they know stuff people don't. Anyway, Lester, he knew somethin' new was up and first chance he gets, he runs off to find everybody.

Anyway, the phone rings and it's Ma and she says, "Dale, that silly old dog has run off. Your Dad didn't want me to tell you, but I thought you should know. Donny loves him so."

"Oh, don't worry about ol' Lester, Ma. He'll show up again soon. Lester's smart even if he looks funny."

Ma laughs, "Well, just thought you should know. How are things?"

"Oh, real good, Ma. Yeah, real good. You and Pop gotta come over here and meet your great grandkids!"

"Oh," she says. "We will! We will! I'm just itching to meet them! So's your dad, but I thought you and Carrie should meet them first."

And I think, ain't that just like Ma and Pop. Don't want to be in the way. Don't want to be a bother. "Well, okay, but we're goin' over to the hospital to see Ike soon. Why don't you come over there?"

"Sure, sure. We'll be right over, Dale. But find that silly dog first."

"Listen, if he's not back by the time we get done with breakfast, I'll come down and look. But them reporters are outside again, five or six of 'em anyway, and they're gonna follow me…"

"Yes. Yes. I heard about that. Darnedest thing! Well, your dad is out looking. Like you say, that silly dog will probably show up soon."

Well, sure enough, he does, but not at Ma and Pop's or at my house, but out at Doc O'Brian's camp! That crazy dog comes out all that way! Knows right where we are. Tracks us! A couple hours later when we're all gettin' ready to go visit Ike at the hospital, I peek out the door and see the reporters are still there, and who is standing there right in the middle of them, but Lester and he's covered in…well…I don't know what all, but let's put it this way, none of them reporters are standin' very close to him. And that gives me a idea.

"Hey Carrie? Is there some rough old soap around or even some shampoo?"

She looks at me funny, but gets it for me. Everybody else is cleaning up and gettin' ready to go and I explain my plan to her and she laughs a long time then says, "Well it's worth a try."

So I'm down in the lake, in a pair of Doc's old swimmin' trunks that don't fit, washin' Lester, who had to be coaxed in with dog biscuits and sure enough all five reporters and a couple camera guys, are gathering' all around askin' me questions. So my plan maybe is workin'. I figured the rest could sneak out while I distracted 'em with this.

"Mr. Sylvanus…Dale…what are you doing?" This woman

reporter, the first one from the press conference I think, asks me.

"Well, I'm washin' Lester."

"Who is Lester?" This same young woman says.

I look at her like it's a stupid question because, well, it is, and she says, "I mean why are you washing your dog now? You've got...guests..."

"Well, miss," I say, "yer welcome to wash Lester for me. I can't take the old fool home unless I wash him first. I can't put him in a car, smellin' like this. See, he walked all the way over here from Hunter and he got himself inta...well...a shit pile on the way..."

It's weird, you know? Here I am explainin' why I'm washin' my dog to a girl I don't know and she's askin' me questions and then all of a sudden everybody comes out of the camp and they all rush to the cars, and I finish up rinsin' Lester and I look up tryin' to see a way I can get through the five or six of 'em and back up to camp. Maybe get Big Ol' to come and pick me up in the wrecker, so I can take Lester back to Ma and Pops or to my house and then head back over to the hospital. And I look up for a minute and Lester takes off on a dead run right through them reporters and camera guys! Even gets tangled in a cable and knocks a camera guy down. The camera goes flyin' and lands on the one reporter's toe and he starts hoppin' around. The family, all of 'em, come out of the house and head for the cars and Lester is runnin' around and around havin' the best time of his life with everybody shoutin' and the other TV camera guy and one of the newspaper guys takin' movies and pictures while the first TV guy tries to pick up his camera and I look up at Donny chasin' Lester around and I catch Dr. Abassi's eye and he is just laughin' so hard and I walk over to him and the one TV camera guy follows me and Dalir looks at me and he just puts his arm around me and says, "Blessings, my friend Dale, blessings."

"Ya..." I say, smilin' back at him, "Doc...I mean Dalir... there's a whole pack a blessings all right. We're...we're lucky fellas." And Carrie tells me later that that runs on the six o'clock news that night.

★★★

Over at the hospital we're havin' a nice get-together. After all the confusion at the O'Brian's camp the reporters are slow in coming down there and when they do it's just the one TV truck and a newspaper reporter from, I think, the Mining Journal in Marquette. She'd just gotten there that day. So, I think, maybe they're startin' to lose interest. And they are, but… Well, other things, that happen later, get'em interested again.

Anyway, by that time they got Ike in a walkin' cast, and we get told that if Carrie can watch him and Donya, and Dorri, for a few days, make sure none of that concussion stuff comes back for any of'em, they should be okay and so we're all fixin' to head over to the house when my phone rings and it's state trooper Teddy Grace.

"Dale, I've been trying not to bother you with all the other stuff going on. Nice work on the rescue, by the way, brother…but I think I might need your help."

"Well…you're right we are pretty busy here…oh…it's Shine, ain't it?"

"Yeah. Somebody broke into the Hunter liquor store last night and I found Shine's Chevy on one of those back roads up north of College Hill about six miles."

"He's got a hunting shack up there…"

"Yeah, I know. There's a couple of the sheriff's boys sitting on that. But he hasn't been there. The FBI's been hanging around the post, but mostly they're just looking important. They don't know this country and Shine could be hiding anywhere. When the city boys tipped me off about the liquor store break-in, I thought maybe Shine might be…"

"Teddy, do you know what's missing from the liquor store?"

"Oh…well I've got a report right here…" I hear him shuffle papers a little. Then he says, "Looks like not that much, four or five bottles of Chivas…"

"It was Shine."

"How do you know?"

"When Shine gets drunk, between all the lies about all the

women he's been with he talks about Chivas. How he wishes he had enough money to get his hands on some Chivas…"

"Okay. So that puts him at the liquor store about 3 a.m. this morning. Probably on foot since he only took five bottles. There hasn't been any cars reported stolen and his Chevy was out of gas."

"And he ain't been to his camp?"

"No."

"Then he's passed out somewhere. About now he's probably waking up."

"Somewhere between the liquor store and his camp. So that puts him in the woods north of town or up on College Hill somewhere."

"Ya, probably."

"Okay. I'm going to have a look both places, but I was wondering if you could take out a half hour and meet me up at St. Ann's. Father Bill said he'd be there a while and he's the only one who's talked to Hughie and Chessy other than cops. I figure maybe they told him something they haven't told us. Might give me a lead on Shine. And then between the two of you, maybe we'll come up with something. Of course I know Father can't tell me anything that was said in confession, or in confidence, but maybe…"

"No worries Teddy, neither one of them jaspers is Catholic anyway…"

Teddy kinda laughs for a second. Then he says, "So can you meet me?"

"Sure, I can sneak away for a fellow Marine."

I turn around and Carrie is just starin' razors at me and I explain it all to her, in one long like sentence. And I'm talkin' in a real accurate way, somehow and all really clear, just the facts, and for a second some part of me wonders where this is comin' from, then, all of a sudden, I know. It's talkin' to Teddy that done it. It put me back in mind of bein' a Marine and havin' a mission. I feel like I really need to do this.

"It'll only be a half hour, hon, and I'll be with Teddy and Father Bill. A guy's life is at stake. I'll grant ya…it ain't much of a life, but I'd just as soon Shine didn't get shot."

Carrie kinda sighs for a second. Finally she says, "God knows that piece of crap wouldn't do this for you, but I guess we can spare you for a half hour. But don't get all mixed up in this, Dale. Shine's made his bed, he'll have to lie in it."

"I know," I say.

I go out and jump in my truck, ignorin' the few reporters still hangin' around. It's only just over a mile from the hospital in the middle of Hunter up the hill to St. Ann's. But the whole way I can't shake that Marine feeling. The streets are real quiet just like they always are on a week day, especially in the summer, but every detail just seems to be jumpin' out at me. When I pull up onto the hill and around the corner, first thing I notice is Teddy's squad car not far from St. Ann's stopped right in the middle of the street with the door still open, but no sign of Teddy. My brain's workin' on overdrive, like I say, almost like from the moment Teddy called I knew somehow that somethin' serious was goin' on. I reach under the seat and grab a tire iron. Wish I had my shotgun, but I don't keep it in the truck after huntin' season. Besides, way I've been livin' up to a day or two ago, havin' a gun in possession just don't make no sense.

I cross the street quick and make my way up the front steps of Saint Ann's. It's not the only building around—there's two or three of the oldest Hunter Woods College buildin's too—but it's the closest one to Teddy's car. I figure, whatever or whoever Teddy was chasin' might of gone in there. It's a pretty big church with two steeples. Whole thing's made out of logs. They built the first part in the 1800's and they added on since usin' logs. Lotta big wigs in the church like to come there cause it's got history.

Anyway, just about the time I open the front doors, I see a news truck pull around the corner. Well, I can't do nothin' about that. Just hope them fools don't get themselves shot. Then it hits me, if this is Shine, would the damned fool have a gun? I hope to Christ not. Because if he does, and he pulls it on Teddy, he's gonna get himself wounded at least, and if there's a hostage involved, Shine's gonna be dead.

So I walk in real quiet to the back of the church and I can't believe what I'm seein'. It's like some kinda show! There's Shine, lookin' plenty the worse for wear and he's got Father Bill around the neck. And it take me a minute, but I can see he's chokin' him with Father's big rosary. Father's eyes look pretty big in a way I ain't never seen'em before and he's tryin' to talk to Shine, but every time he does, Shine chokes him again.

And right up on the altar with them, just a couple of steps away is Teddy, and thank God he don't have his gun out, but he does have his hand on the butt of it, and he's talkin' real calm to Shine too.

I stand up straight, and I just start walkin' down the aisle and there in the middle of it is a half drunk bottle of Chivas.

I pick it up and keep walkin' without slowin' down.

"Semper fi," I say out loud.

Teddy glances my way for a second. "Semper fi, Dale."

"What you want, Sylvanus? You fuckin' traitor!"

"All I want is for you to let the priest go, Shine."

"No way. He's my only way out of here." He chokes Father again, and I can see Father can't talk he's choking so hard. I gotta do something right now.

"You got no way outta here, Shine." I say. "You're goin' to prison. And if you don't listen to me, you may be goin' to the cemetery."

"How you figure?"

"Well, Teddy ain't just a state cop, Shine. He was a Marine sharpshooter. They don't come any better than that. And if you don't let Father go, I figure you got about half a minute before Teddy takes the shot. I know he's already got it lined up. Ain't that right, Teddy?"

Teddy's got the gun out now and he's got it trained on Shine, "Semper Fuckin' fi."

Shine all of a sudden looks even more scared than a second ago.

I say, "I'll make you a deal, though. You turn the priest over to me and I'll give you what's left of the Chivas. I figure Teddy'll

probably let you finish it before he takes you in.
How about it Teddy."

"Sounds like a plan."

Shine's little pig eyes are just dancin' in his head and finally he says. "Chivas first!"

I hold out the bottle and walk pretty close to him.

"Give me the priest or no Chivas. You better take the deal 'cause your thirty seconds are about up."

Shine gives me one last look, cusses, and lets Father go. Father takes a big gasp of air and staggers towards me. I notice he takes a glance at the bottle of Chivas as I slide it across the altar to Shine. Teddy walks a little closer and stands there for fifteen seconds while Shine empties the bottle, then cuffs him.

By now I got a hold of Father, and Teddy finishes reading Shine his rights.

"Can you fellas stop down at the post later, so we can fill out some papers? No hurry."

"Sure," I say.

"You okay, Father?" I ask.

He looks at me and for just a second I hardly recognize him, he looks so scared and kind of small. Just an old man. It makes me feel bad.

"Let's get out of here, Dale." he says.

Teddy says, "Might want to get checked out at the hospital, Father."

Father turns and looks at Teddy, I can see the life comin' back into his eyes very fast. Them white eyebrows kinda lower, and he looks real sharp at both of us. I smile a little at him, but his look doesn't change and he says real slow and careful like, "Jesus, Mary, and Joseph you boys! Don't you know old priests only go to hospitals as visitors? And we seldom stay long. There's no point in giving anyone any ideas. And I've got lots of God's work still to do!" He looks up at the cross and crosses himself and makes one of them genuflections, so I do the same.

I can see the spark is back in Father, so I'm not worried. A hundred and fifty Shines couldn't take that old man down. I turn with him towards the back of the church and there they are: a camera crew. I find out later, they caught the whole. Deal. Father grabs my sleeve and leads me behind the altar and out into the alley. Just before we leave I hear Teddy call out, "Well done, Marine."

★★★

So, here we are, Father and me headin' back down the hill into town. One TV truck is behind us, but I don't even try to shake'em. And as soon as we get back down the hill, all of a sudden, I just start laughin' my ass off and I can't stop. Tears runnin' down after a while. Father starts laughin' with me. Finally I say, "That... that was a helluva thing. Oh...oh sorry Father."

Father, who's lookin' a little worse for wear again maybe because he's had some time to think about it all, says, "You know what?"

I look over at him, "What Father?"

"When you were standing there holding out that bottle to Shine, it looked pretty good to me too. They don't pay me enough."

We both start laughin' again, and we can't stop and we just keep rollin' down that street.

One week ago, one week ago, who coulda thought this is where I'd be, this is what I'd be doin'. I keep thinkin' I'm gonna wake up and this is all gonna be a dream. It sure as hell seems like it.

★★★

At the hospital back in Hunter, Jen is standin' there in the parking lot waiting for me. She's laughin' when she sees me. She holds out her cell phone and shows me some new headline, "Hero Marine Saves the Day Again."

"Oh Lord..." I say.

"That's my line," Father says.

"You okay, Father?" Jen asks. "Do you want to get checked out?"

"No." Father says, and there's ice in it.

I wink at Jen and she nods.

About then the TV truck that's been following us is unloading and the reporter is trying to get us to wait and do an interview and Jen takes over and waves us toward the building. We go as quick as we can. The TV reporter is shoutin' questions and Jen is tryin' to keep him from coming inside after us, but he'll be inside soon, no doubt.

And after all that, once we get inside, Father Bill kinda takes a breath. He takes me out into the little chapel at the end of the hall in the hospital, partly to pray, but partly just to be away from it all for a second. And after we both kneel down and pray for a second or two he sits back in the pew. I see a look in his eyes I ain't never seen before. And he tries to say something about ten times and then, he just starts cryin'. So, I wait for him to stop. Then, I take him out through the kitchen, out to my truck, and thank God the reporter from TV and any others that might have caught up with him ain't there, and we hop in and without even thinkin' about where we're goin' I start drivin' and he finally looks up and he says, "Oh Dale, I've been through a lot of things in my life, but I've never been that scared."

"Well that's…just sensible, Father. Anybody'd be scared. Shine's got no sense and well…he mighta killed ya. He's always scared me that way."

"No, no you don't get it. When you held out that bottle to Shine, for just a second I thought it was for me. And I wanted to drink that whole bottle, Dale. I would have if Shine hadn't taken it. I almost slugged him to get it when he let me go."

I nod and think about that for a second. "So…so is there a…what…a sponsor you need to talk to, some place I can take you…"

"Yeah…"

I look at Father and almost say "Where?" but he heads me off.

"I want to go fishing. I've been a fisher of men enough for one day."

So, in the middle of all this, after all we've both been through this week, Father and I go out to the lake. I call Carrie from the truck on speaker. She already knows about it all since it's on TV. She asks if Father doesn't want to get checked out, and

Father, does this kinda deep angry what...sigh...and I tell her no, he's definitely okay. So she says that I should go ahead and fish with him. Then she says, "Men are idiots. Even priests." I try not to laugh out loud. But Father does it for me and says, "Especially priests, Carrie."

To shake them reporters, though I don't think any of them are followin' probably too busy tryin' to get the story out before we get there, I drive on back roads and a muddy two track with a log bridge over the swamp around to the west of the lake where they can't follow, just to make sure. Father don't need no questions right now. Neither do I. It puts me in mind of me and the other jarheads after patrols in Iraq. We just wanted to talk to each other, if we was gonna talk at all. Nobody else would understand anyway.

I get out Pop's old wooden boat from a cove way on the far side of the lake, and we go fishin'. And it's clear and it's calm. Just what Father needs. Me too, I guess.

And I watch Father and he just kinda breathes in and out and looks up at the sky and a time or two. He is sweatin' and prayin' and then a little sprinkle of rain comes and he starts to laugh with tears still in his eyes. And he just looks at me and he says, "Grace, Dale. That's what you call Grace. The intervention of Heaven in our lives. It was close there for a bit, but He always comes through if I pay attention."

And he laughs and he looks over at me and really I don't know what to make of what he says not even a little bit and he says, "Do you know what this makes you, Dale?"

And I shake my head.

"My confessor."

"I don't know what that means."

"It doesn't matter, Dale. You are anyway."

"What do I have to do? To be a...what's it?"

"Confessor. What you just did. Take me fishing when I ask you."

"Well...hell...that's not much."

The tears well up on him again, "There you go, Dale, underestimating yourself again. All the best ones do that."

He grins at me, puts his finger to his lips to keep me from talkin' and looks out at his line.

★★★

That night about 8 or so, we're back out at O'Brian's camp. After all that mess at St. Ann's, the reporters are camped now, I mean really camped. They got three sleeping tents down in the front yard by the lake and a little screened tent with our picnic table inside and everything.

Father and Mr… Dr….Dalir cooked this up together. Instead of tryin' to avoid'em, the two of them just figure to kill'em with kindness until it all blows over. So Father got the tents from St. Ann's, they use'em for outings with the college kids.

So the reporters got a little camp. There's about ten in all now, from about five different papers, and radio, and TV, whatnot. One from CNN, but the rest mostly local. And they're still takin' pictures and film and what not, but they don't know what to do about us answerin' all their questions and just bein' nice to'em. Hell, Pop's down there tellin'em tales and the Abassies and Carrie and Ma, who is lovin' them great grand children all to distraction, are even bringin'em food! And Jen says, "Well, that's not the weirdest approach I've ever seen to the media, but I guess; it's the nicest. They must feel like they're in the Presidential reporter's pool. If we can just keep something else from happening for the next couple days, maybe they'll all go away."

"If they don't," Dalir says, and flashes his little smile, "we shall just keep being kind."

I laugh and say, "Or we can just real gradual like cut their rations."

Later on, Carrie corners me in the camp kitchen and asks me about the book, "Given it any more thought?"

"It is a lotta money."

"Only if it's Jen though, right?"

"Right." I say.

"You sure? It'll be a lot less if she does it from what Jen says. And she wants us both to write it all out so we don't feel like we're bein' misquoted."

"I can't write nothin'…"

"Sure you can! I'll help, and so will Jen, but it would be a lot more money if we just let somebody interview us and then let them go to it."

I say, "Would you trust anybody else? Is all that money worth anything if they write a bunch of lies?"

"Father tell you to say that?"

"Well…not directly…but yeah, I think so."

"You're a smart man, Dale."

"No. No I ain't, but I'm me, and I guess, after you kinda sift through all the stuff all these crazy people are sayin' about you and me and our family this week, I guess maybe bein' me ain't that bad."

Carrie tears up, "I've got the best husband in the world."

I laugh, "You keep tellin' yourself that, hon. Maybe you can stick with me until I screw up again."

"You know what?" She says. "I think I will." And she kisses me right there in front of everybody. And I look over and the kids don't even notice 'cause they're havin' a great time. And Donya and Ike are holding hands on a couch, him with his foot propped up and her just holdin' her little belly and smilin' at Ike.

"It's nice to see young people in love, isn't it?" Carrie says.

"Ya," I say. "'Specially when they're our young people."

And Farrin and Dalir and Father are playin' Michigan Rummy with Donny and Dorri and Kelly out on the front porch. And my Ma and Pop are kinda lookin' in over their great granddaughter's hand and helpin' and Donny says, "Hey, no fair!" And everybody laughs.

"It's…it's a good life, Carrie." I say, just kinda watchin' it all.

"Thanks to you."

"No, thanks to God's Grace."

"Now I know Father told you that."

"Maybe," I say. "But he just read it in some old book."

That makes Carrie laugh kinda gentle like and she hugs me.

And the night goes on and it gets darker in that camp and

the voices get quieter and quieter. And pretty soon the kids are sleepin', kinda leanin' in on each other, and by this time Ma and Pop are playin' serious euchre with Father and the Abbasies and Carrie. And Lester is out there too snorin' away on the floor when he's not lookin' for a handout. Even the reporters have gone home except for that one young woman from the Mining Journal who must be reading in her tent 'cause I see a little light there, and I can hear a loon callin' out on the lake. And I hear Pop explainin' what it is to Dorri and not to be afraid. And he starts tellin' all about'em and how long they live and how he's seen this and that with'em, stories I heard a thousand times before. Stories that get better with the re-tellin'. Oh I don't know. It's just…it's just a really good night is all. I don't know what else to say.

Epilogue

Saturday, 7:32 a.m.

That word, "epilogue", well it ain't one a mine. Jen says that's what you write when the story is over and you just have to write up all the details that kinda close it out. This wasn't really wrote on that Saturday, but 7:32 is when I got up…Saturday morning… and I wrote the rest like days of the week so I figured I better finish this way. Jen can put it any way she wants. I trust her. There ain't much more to tell. And if I'd a thought about it more when Carrie first mentioned it to me, that Jen was gonna make me do all this work writin' all this stuff down, instead'a just tellin' her, so she could write her book about us, I don't think I woulda gone along with it. Somethin' about gettin' the voice just right with the facts or somethin'. Don't really know what she means by "voice". Seems like the voice would go better if I was talkin', but what do I know? But, anyway, it's a lotta money for a lotta people I love, and some for the church too, though Father Bill didn't ask for none, so I guess it's worthwhile. By the way I gotta say Father Bill is one a them people I love too. He's kinda like a brother now, not like a brother from the church, but like my own brother, the one I ain't never had. A good one. A older one. One that tells ya stuff ya can take or leave and some that you can take to the bank for truth, and he don't hold it against ya whatever ya do, but bawls ya out when ya need it and pats your back when ya got it comin' and never does neither one when ya don't need it, if ya know what I mean.

Anyway, the way this all ends up is this: the reporters and all the news about us was done after another two or three days, a bunch of press conferences and a lotta bein' nice. Jen told me ol' Shakespeare called what we was doin', "...patient merit of the unworthy..." I wrote that down so I could put it here. She also says this story is a story of what another writer, Hemingway, called, "grace under pressure." Well, I think the only people had Grace under pressure in this story was Carrie and Father, and maybe Teddy too, but they don't agree with me; they think I'm the hero, so I'm just kinda goin' along.

Along the way it come out from Teddy and the feds what happened with Shine. After he ran away from the border that night he ditched his Chevy when it run out of gas up by his shack where Teddy found it. The feds had a report out to look out for him at the Mackinac Bridge and down state, but Teddy figured, and he figured right, that Shine weren't that smart and probably would just head home like a wounded bear. And he did, but he was smart enough not to take the highway. He took every back rode between Hunter and the Soo, and there's a lot of them. Well, they already had Shine's shack staked out by the time Shine got there, so he run off in the woods on foot until he got thirsty, then snuck into town on foot and broke into the liquor store down town in Hunter. Like I say, Shine ain't no rocket scientist so he started in on them bottles right away as he was walkin' back up College Hill for the woods north of town and passed out in the alley between St. Ann's and one of college buildings. Well, the damn fool was staggerin' around in broad daylight just when Teddy pulled up next morning. Shine run into St. Ann's, then, where Father was puttering around waiting for Teddy and me to show up, and...well...you know the rest.

As for Hughie and Chessy, well they both testified against Shine. They told Teddy and the feds everything they could think of about where Shine might be, so their sentence went a little lighter. It also helped that they wasn't the one that punched and kicked the customs officer to begin with, and that they stayed at the scene and didn't resist arrest. I wonder if they only stayed at the scene because Shine was faster than they were, and took off before they could get in the car, but I ain't never asked them. Anyway, they'll probably even see the light of day after a while. I don't know if Shine's gonna be that lucky. I don't know if he should be that lucky either.

The Abbasies went home, but they promised to come back to see what Fall and Winter are like and we promised to go out west, and we can, with the money from the book. And, oh yeah, I forgot the most important part, Ike and Donya and the kids have moved to Hunter! After all the hubbub was done, which nobody in town liked, we invited the town people out to the lake and we had a big blowout at the end of the summer and everybody talked about what a crazy time it was and how glad they were to have Ike back and how nice Donya is and one thing led to another and, well there was a openin' for a "professor of international studies" whatever in the world that is (truth, I think some a them folks at the college made it up so they could keep Donya around) and Donya jumped at the chance since it was a couple steps up from her job in Oregon, and soon as Ike's leg gets better they're puttin' him on at the college too to assistant manage the maintenance and maybe take over when Rich Aho retires next year. What's more he gets to be a "guest lecturer" in the art department, whatever that means, and he's gonna keep right on sellin' his pots in stores out in Oregon, in a couple local stores, and online. Damned if they didn't offer me a job too, but I turned 'em down. Just thought they was bein' nice and besides, now that I ain't a drunken fool crashin' into everything and everybody all the time, I got lots of things to do, and the GI Bill helps, and now all the money from the book.

Jen says, "It's all pretty contrived" and that them folks at the college might just be hopin' to capitalize on the book, to get some more kids at the school and raise funds and all that, and she kinda got all worked up.

Well, I don't understand and I kinda forget she ain't family exactly and I look at her and say, "What the hell's the matter with that, Jen? Ike's got a job; you got the best writing project ya ever had; my folks are so proud they're about to bust, and Carrie cries all the time she's so happy. What's more, I'm gettin' along with my kids, and the kids look like they're goin' places, though Donny's gonna have to get over bein' famous and expectin' it to ever happen again, and Kelly just needs to be careful with that Chesterfield boy, though he seems a good enough sort. And, well, the grand kids are just…just about the best thing goin'. So what's the big deal if the college folks helped the family out a little and in return make a little cash for the school and the town? What in the hell is the matter with that?"

So anyway, Carrie is there, with Jen and me in our kitchen when this all comes up, and Carrie just busts out laughin' at the look on Jen's face and the way I shut her right down, the way nobody in town ever does, without even meanin' to really.

And then Jen busts out too and says, "You know what, Dale? I guess you're right. Nothing is the matter with that. I guess I better just shut up for once and let you folks be happy."

And that's what we are. It's pretty simple really. I don't know if this all happened so this could work out this way, and Father won't give me no straight answer about that, except to say, "What do you think?" Like he always does. But I guess, after all, it don't matter. We are where we are and it's good right now. I ain't the brightest fella in the world, but they all got me convinced I ain't the dumbest neither. So I feel kinda free, after all this writin', to say that I think maybe bein' happy right where ya are, right now… well…maybe that's all anybody should ever worry about.

Acknowledgements

Thank you to Editor-in-Chief, Matt Dryer and Book Editors Lindsay Brindley, Monica Nordeen and Shantel Dryer; the folks at Snowbound Books, The Marquette Regional History Center, Uptown Gifts, Snyder's, Da Yoopers Tourist Trap, Falling Rock Cafe and Books, U.P. Trading Company, Peter White Public Library, Bayliss Public Library, The Marquette Mining Journal, The Sault Evening News, TV 6 and 10 Marquette, and all other media outlets who helped with publicity; Tyler Tichelaar and the folks of Marquette Monthly: Tom Powers and the folks of Michigan in Books: Lisa Barry and the folks of WEMU; Shelley Russell, Beverly Matherne, and Marty Achatz of Northern Michigan University, and Helen Haskell Remien of The Joy Center; those who have followed the book announcements and publicity on tumblr at bgbradleyauthor.tumblr.com and all those who have followed the poetry, book excerpts and random thoughts for the last year and a half on the Facebook page: North Words with Beeg; and last, but certainly not least, my colleagues, students, fans, friends, and my loving family. This book exists because of each and every one of you. On we go!

ABOUT THE AUTHOR

B.G. BRADLEY is a retired high school teacher, former newspaper reporter and columnist, part time college professor, poet, novelist, playwright, director and actor. His fiction, non-fiction, and poetry have appeared in various regional publications including *Detroit Sunday Magazine, Michigan Out-of-Doors, Passages North, Sidewalks, Foxcry Review, The Marquette Mining Journal,* and *The Newberry News.* His plays have appeared on local stages including the Lake Superior Theatre which in 2010 produced his *Lake Stories,* the Hunter Lake books, which he wrote, directed, and starred in as Ben O'Brian opposite NMU's Dr. Shelley Russell as Grace. Bradley lives in Diorite with the love of his life, Debbie, and his labrador, Tom. His sons Taggart and Patrick are actors and arts activists on their own.

Coming in 2019:
Fallback

The third installment in the Hunter Lake series by B.G. Bradley!

Jake is back in town! Jake O'Brian, the home town kid, the Hunter boy who made good, the former star athlete and scholar who became an international lawyer with a reputation for brilliance and charm, is back in Hunter. Jake O'Brian, who only recently married Christy, the young, beautiful girl from Reno, after all those years moving from one lovely woman to the next, is back in Hunter...alone.

He thinks nobody knows, but this is Hunter, and Jake's younger sister Jen lives here and she always gets the scoop. Jake's older brother Ben is here and he would know the shiny signs of his younger brother anywhere. Jake is back, and it's no secret.

Come along with us back to Hunter, Michigan, the small town near the beautiful lake and the wild river, with the wooded hills and valleys, where everyone has the heart for long winters and their eyes are always looking towards short lovely summers, cold springs, and enchanting falls.

Fall back into this world with Jake, Ben, Val , Michael and Kate Jen, Mark and their boys, the Slyvanuses old and new and all the other folks around Hunter. Fall back into the magic and mystery of small town life. Fall back into this world you already know, but still can know much better. We've only scratched the surface so far. Winter and Summer are never the full story here. Fall back where the waters run deep and slow and show you complexities few, who live elsewhere, believe could be part of a small rural town.

Join us for *Fallback* the third Hunter Lake novel in 2019!

96538031R00095

Made in the USA
Columbia, SC
30 May 2018